THE TWO MUJERES

THE TWO MUJERES

by Sara Levi Calderón

translated by Gina Kaufer

aunt lute books
SAN FRANCISCO

Translated by Gina Kaufer;
revisions by the author for the English version

First Edition
10-9-8-7-6-5-4-3-2-1

Aunt Lute Books
P.O Box 410687
San Francisco, CA 94141

Cover and Text Design: Pam Wilson Design Studio
Cover Art: Chris Tandy
Editor: Joan Pinkvoss
Production: Martha Davis
             Jayna Brown
Typesetting: Debra DeBondt

Printed in the U.S.A on acid-free paper

This book is an Aunt Lute Foundation educational project.

This is a work of fiction. In no way does it intend to represent any real person, living or dead, or any real incidents.

Library of Congress Cataloging-in-Publication Data

Calderón, Sara Levi, 1942-
     [Dos mujeres.   English]
     The two mujeres / by Sara Levi Calderón ; translated by
Gina Kaufer. — 1st ed.
         p.   cm.
     Translation of: Dos mujeres.
     ISBN 1-879960-01-X (lib. bdg.) : $18.95 —
ISBN 1-879960-00-1 (pbk. : acid-free paper) : $8.95
     I. Title.
PQ7298.A29D613   1991
863—dc20   91-21444
                                                      CIP

ACKNOWLEDGMENTS

My special thanks to Joan Pinkvoss, my editor for the warm, intelligent and professional help she provided to improve this novel. I also thank Jayna Brown and Martha Davis for giving their knowledge and energy to the difficult task of editing a text written in a different language.

I thank my translator, Gina Kaufer; my severest critic, yet always honest and clear concerning the literary purposes I have pursued in this work.

I also thank Tede Matthews, the impetus for the translation of *Dos Mujeres*, for his unwavering support of Latino culture.

My wish has been to tell the story of a woman's life which could have been mine as well.

When the Macedonians
abandoned him and proved that they preferred
Pyrrhus, King Demetrius—he had a great soul—did
not, so they stated, behave in the least like a King.
He took off his robes of gold and cast off his purple
shoes. He dressed hurriedly in simple clothes and
left like an actor who, when the performance is
over, changes his clothes and departs.

The King Demetrius
Constantin Cavafy
translated by Rae Dalven
Harvest/HBJ book, 1976

to Gina with love

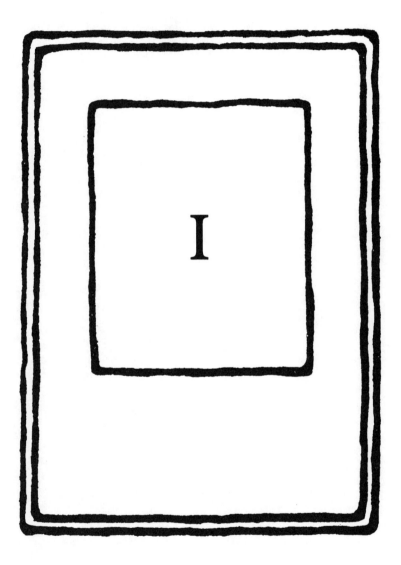

I

THE GRAY SNAKE

The car was racing at a steady pace. It seemed time had stopped. The road was like a huge gray snake splitting the red clay earth of Michoacán.

She took a joint out of her big black purse and asked if I wanted to smoke.

"Driving?"

"Yes, why not?"

"You're right, why not?"

I was fascinated by the sensations that marijuana produced. It helped me focus in on my thoughts, it sharpened my ear, my skin; everything attained presence.

She was looking at the road, immersed in a world I knew nothing of. A year before, as I was boarding the plane at De Gaulle Airport, I had invited her to be my guest if she ever came back to México.

"Are you serious?" she had asked with tears in her eyes.

"Absolutely."

She had said she would certainly consider it. Now she was 'back home,' as she used to say ironically. Life had been terribly difficult for her in this past year.

Morena wanted to know how I was feeling. "Just perfect," I replied, and we laughed. I slowed down at last, and began to enjoy her company and the view. Lush soft hills with white adobe houses lay scattered here and there; bougainvillea and *llamaradas* were everywhere.

"You know what? I have the feeling you could spoil me," I said. She burst out laughing.

"Shouldn't it be the other way around?"

Our difference in age made me old enough to be her mother. But we never talked about that.

I looked at her with tenderness.

3

"What is it?" she asked.

"Nothing, just looking."

We arrived in Pátzcuaro as the sun was setting. She didn't feel like staying in one of the plush hotels and suggested something 'more indigenous.' I had no objections; on the contrary, the idea attracted me. Even though life was hard on her, Morena was a symbol of freedom to me.

We walked into the Janitzio Hotel, painted in blue *añil* and smelling of bidet. As we were asking for a room, we heard a harsh voice claiming that Lupita was a *pendeja*. When I turned to look, I saw a green plucked *loro* that repeated its little phrase over and over again.

I was starved. I asked Morena if we could leave our luggage in the room and look for something to eat right away. She suggested we go to the plaza. We entered the *zócalo* as the birds began singing in the foliage.

I noticed three bulls' heads lying on a green wrought-iron bench, dripping blood on the pavement. I turned away, horrified.

"See that?" I cried out.

"Yes," she answered calmly. "What's the big deal? They're only heads torn from their bodies."

"And so what. Do you see this every day of your life?"

"No, but that's what you see in México."

"And that's the reason it doesn't move you?... well, well..."

A man in a white apron smeared with blood approached the bench. He tied the horns of the heads together and left with them hanging from his shoulders. That was the end of the bloody show.

Morena wanted *una sopita caliente*, a plate of hot soup. At the other end of the plaza she glimpsed a food stall. I let her lead me there knowing that my prudishness was a result of my education, and for three days I wanted to be free of it. Morena ordered a plate of bone marrow soup, *un taco de buche y otro de ojo*. As I watched the food being prepared, I felt sick, walked away and threw up.

The next day we were on the road again. We headed for Santa Clara del Cobre to visit her friend Ana, an heiress to famous poets. Ana was a proud Mexican beauty with dark hair and deep dark eyes. She worked as a coppersmith, like the majority of people in this mining town.

4

Santa Clara had been chosen to forge gigantic copper jewels as a present from the Mexican government for the Statue of Liberty's Centennial. Ana had been appointed head of the project. Her inventiveness was wild. The ring of the Lady could be strapped around the waist of an elephant.

She was also helping the townswomen organize for better wages and living conditions. She had become a public figure. "The men don't like me here," she said. "They're trying to frighten me out. But I'm stubborn, and I'm giving them a hell of a time."

"And how's your uncle David?" she asked Morena. He had been her first husband and the greatest love of her youth.

"He's fine, and how about you?" Morena wanted to know. Ana said she was happy at last; she had married again. She asked Morena about Genovesa. "Yes, she's still painting and she's still with Raúl...but not for long," Morena said.

"*Ay, las cosas del corazón,*" Ana crooned, her hair falling back, revealing her bare shoulders.

The next day she came to Pátzcuaro to have dinner with us. She was dressed with Parisian elegance.

The evening was simply delightful.

JOURNEYS ARE DREAMS

As we drove through the outskirts of the city, I invited Morena to have lunch at my house. I never used to ask her home because my sons thought she was weird. "Why is she always wearing *huaraches?*" they would ask. "Doesn't she have any money to buy shoes?" They despised her looks and they couldn't understand why she was my friend.

Morena stared at me. "Aren't you scared of going back?"

"I'm not scared, I'm panicked."

"Always so frank," she said.

We laughed so hard that tears came to our eyes. The Michoacán air still lingered in our lungs and we were *chapeadas,* our cheeks a healthy red.

When we got to my house the boys were already having lunch. I kissed them both and Morena asked the usual *¿cómo están?* They answered in monosyllables: okay, fine.

We sat at the table and María Luisa served us lunch. She came from a ranch near El Oro.

"We were not far from there," I told her. "All of Michoacán is beautiful, especially its people."

She smiled happily and asked Morena if she had liked it as much as I had. Morena answered that she had liked it even more and they both laughed.

My sons urged María Luisa to bring in their meat plates.

"I'm going, I'm going, *joven* Alberto," she said, already walking into the kitchen with the rhythmic movement of her big hips. Ricky called out for her to bring the *Excélsior.*

"Since when do you read the newspaper at the table?" I asked.

"Since now," he answered, not looking at me.

When Morena and I were back in my room, I explained to her that my children were very jealous concerning their mother. "It's nothing personal against you," I assured her.

6

"But certainly," she replied. "How could they not like me?"

"That's true."

"So you mean to say they're only as jealous as one would expect them to be? Well, I've got news for you. I'm certain they're just keeping face. They wouldn't want their friends to see you in bad company, right?" she said sarcastically.

"You're absolutely right. It's a class issue."

As I said this, Crispina, my son's dog, came in wagging her tail. I stroked the long white hairs on her neck and held her head against my face. She was a beautiful collie that I had bought Ricky as a present a few months before.

Watching this affectionate exchange, Morena remarked that she'd better leave. She said her aunt would kill her if she didn't get home by tonight.

I went downstairs with her to help her pick up her things and say goodbye. We wouldn't be seeing each other until I finished my thesis. That had been the deal before we started our trip, since I had to hand in my paper before the holiday was over.

A GLANCE AT MY ROOMS

Two weeks later, I was finishing the final draft of my sociology thesis, which meant the end of my days as a student. And now what? I asked myself. Am I going to sit in an office, producing bulky bundles of papers that will fill me with vanity and no one will read? Obviously, I had confined myself inside the study for too long and needed some fresh air. I looked for the family album that I kept in one of the desk drawers. I often had the need to go back and search into my blood ties.

Not long ago, I had discovered a treasure, a series of photographs that had belonged to my grandmother. I found a picture of two old-fashioned beauties, my grandmother and my mother, at a time in their lives when they still believed age couldn't leave its mark on their faces. They thought youth was eternal and ay! I myself suffered from this misconception. It was a vice that ran in my female heritage. During my entire life I'd consciously tried to avoid worrying about aging; I tried to be different, to become a self-sufficient, thinking woman. But now that I was about to turn thirty-nine, I couldn't help feeling that the golden age of my youth was ending. The power conferred by beauty would only be a memory for the album.

I recalled the words of my friend Chalo when he talked about women over forty. "They horrify me," he used to say, this little monster, over fifty-six himself... aj!

I looked at my hands; I had recently developed ugly spots on them. *Flores de panteón* we call them in Spanish: 'cemetery flowers.'

Rage burst from my left temple. Furious, I hurled the photographs to the floor, then tried to stop the album from falling but it was too late. I had also knocked over a vase filled with roses and water on top of my visual legacy. And I did nothing to rescue it.

I got up from the desk that had welcomed my thoughts for hours and massaged my buttocks with a circular motion. I started up the stairs. Out of habit, I counted every step: one, two...eight, nine, ten to the landing. Bougainvillea crawled over the white-washed wall, a furtive stream of light stole in from the skylight. I was disturbed by the crazy game of talking to myself.

I continued to climb until I reached the twentieth step. I pushed the bedroom door but it refused to open. I leaned my full weight against it until it finally gave way. Ah! what a surprise: order reigned inside. It seemed like someone else's space. I glanced at myself in the mirror across the room and pulled back the flaccid skin of my face with my hands. Unexpectedly, my father came to mind. "It's me, father. I, who would have been your legitimate pride if I had been male."

I lit a cigarette and walked pensively to the railing. The bedroom was like a large loft that overlooked the study and from there I could see the puddle of spilled water. I turned on the switch of the merry-go-round downstairs. The superb dance started. Reflected in the angled bedroom mirror, the three carved wooden horses became six. I flung the cigarette into the puddle and wondered if I would ever have the courage to throw myself down those ten feet.

As I visualized the horrible scene, the phone rang. It was Morena. She wanted to know how I was feeling. Was I still alive? Had I finished my work?

"I'm all right," I said, "I'm just waiting for the love of my life."

"So you're still waiting?"

"Why, do you think I'm too old to find it?"

"Would a magic wand help?" she corrected herself.

"And what if my evil serpents come out?"

"Wow! serpents? Don't worry, I'll show you how to use it."

She was calling to invite me to an amateur play; Genovesa and her ex-husband would be going too.

"No, sorry, I don't feel like picking up my mood for the benefit of strangers. Besides, I have another appointment."

"So cancel it!" she said promptly.

"All right, but pick me up on time. You know I hate to be kept waiting."

LA CASA DEL LAGO

I suggested we take a walk around the lake. There was a full moon shining on the water and everything under its light appeared motionless. I turned to look at Morena; she was staring absently. I wondered if she was recalling the frightful clinic where human intelligence was considered disposable and lobotomies were performed with the families' consent. Images flooded my brain: grief-stricken Christs hanging from white walls, emaciated nurses keeping order.

Morena turned her eyes on me. She had the appearance of a little girl caught up in some mischief.

"Don't go back to Paris," I pleaded.

"I have to. You know I promised Marta I would go back. She has to believe it's possible to go clean, to 'get off the horse.'"

To me, Marta was just a story with no face, and even so I hated her. I had the foreboding that Morena would go back to drugs when she returned.

We left the bench where we were sitting, held hands and spun around and around until we were dizzy.

"I'm going to miss you," I said.

"I'm going to miss you too."

I invited her to walk along the tree-lined alleys. Far in the distance, the city lights looked like fluorescent threads. Birds trilled and the trees turned to shadows on the pavement.

The imperishable chess players were sprinkled around long log tables, playing quietly.

"Checkmate!" The husky voice seemed to emerge from the underworld. This fraction of a second made me suddenly aware of death, and I suffered.

Morena sensed something, drew an indigo scarf from inside her black purse and swirled it round her neck. She slipped an arm through mine and said, "It's time."

In the dark, La Casa del Lago was an enchanted palace. Like tired gazelles we climbed the stairs to the main entrance. Inside, a chandelier with yellow-tinted lamps suffused the atmosphere with pale calm.

There was a young couple standing in the marble hall observing our arrival. When the woman saw me she pulled her hands out of her pants' pockets. I pulled mine out too.

We both smiled.

Morena introduced me to Genovesa; her cousin was a painter. She had a strange beauty. The man had a long beard and very black eyes.

Genovesa opened the conversation, asking about our trip to Michoacán. Morena described our meeting with Ana in Santa Clara; she told her what Ana was doing there, about her relationship with her new husband, and especially about the charming dinner we had had together at the lake of Pátzcuaro.

I added some piquant details that seemed to please the cousin. She kept observing me with a puzzled look. Surely she's asking herself why a much older woman is friends with her young cousin, I thought.

Meanwhile, destiny was scheming around us. A skeletal woman stuck her head out from behind the wine-colored drapes and announced with a shaky voice that the play had to be cancelled for reasons beyond their control.

Genovesa dropped her eyes and stared at the yellowish wooden planks of the floor. Raúl nervously shifted his weight from one foot to the other.

"And what are you all planning to do now?" he asked, concerned.

Genovesa raised her eyes and sighed. "Us all? Let's stay together as we had planned to," she said, her head to one side as though wondering if her sentence was well constructed.

For a minute I worried that the invitation was not inclusive, but then she asked if I agreed to her proposal. My nod was so firm it made her laugh.

They started looking for the best place to have drinks. We were an unusual group and it was obviously difficult to make a decision. My house would be the perfect place, I thought, but I knew that strangers always found it excessive; too…something.

My tongue untied as I thought about that. "I think we can find what you're all looking for in my house."

My lofty style raised doubts in Genovesa's mind, so she turned to look at her cousin. Morena confirmed my words with a nod.

We were the last to leave La Casa del Lago.

THE CARROUSEL

We walked across the stone-paved road, circled round the fountain and went through a heavily carved door to my studio. I switched on the lights, turning the dimmers down. They slipped like nymphettes into my world. They watched me closely; I felt on display, *como pájaro en la mira.*

Raúl seemed to find everything out of this world, prodigious; she only watched and was silent. The eucalyptus were swaying violently on the terrace. A flock of pigeons came swooping by and I playfully said they were sea gulls. "Oh, we're so near the ocean?" she asked, her eyes laughing.

The first thing we learned about each other was that we were passionate for the sea.

Raúl went to the carrousel, glanced at it, bewildered, and asked if it worked. I pushed the studio button that turned it on. The three wooden horses went up and down their poles, the smiles of old weary goddesses carved on their muzzles.

"It's magical!" she cried out at last. Instinctively, her gaze drifted to the reflection in the mirrors. She fixed her eyes on me and an electric surge, starting in my skull, rushed down my spine until it reached my sex. "Wonderful," she repeated.

Raúl wanted to know where I had found this beautiful piece of craftsmanship.

"It's a violent story," I replied. "In one of my visits to Oaxaca, I found the carrousel rotting in an empty lot next to the town fair. I was told that a young man, madly in love with his brother's wife, shot them both as they were riding on the same wooden horse. The merry-go-round was left to weather until I came to its rescue, years later. I restored it and here it is for the pleasure of us all," I said, inviting them to sit in front of the fireplace.

Raúl chose the cushions scattered on the rug. Genovesa sensed she was being observed by me and couldn't find her place.

She looked up and pointed to the balcony above us. "What's up there?" she asked.

"It's my bedroom. There's also a large terrace outside where I do my gardening." She said that my house seemed like it had popped out of a dream.

"Actually it did," I said. "For years I dreamed I had discovered a house underneath my real house. I had to walk down fearsome subterranean hallways to reach it but when I finally did, everything seemed wonderful and I was happy. When I decided to build this house I tried to reconstruct the images that I had obsessively dreamed."

"And did your dreams come true?" Genovesa asked sarcastically.

"As far as the house goes, they did. But happiness…well, that's hard to say."

I walked over to the fireplace and built a tower of firewood with lots of *ocote*. The fire roared high in a second. Genovesa was amazed at my skills.

"What, are you prejudiced against women of my class?"

"I am," she admitted openly with a smile.

Raúl, who didn't take his eyes off her, passed her a lit cigarette.

Morena had been sitting absent-mindedly on the fireplace step. She dipped her hand into her famous big black purse and extracted some scented weed. "May I?" she asked.

I was about to say no, fearing my sons' return, but I thought they surely wouldn't trust me if I did. So without missing a beat I said, "Of course you may, go ahead."

We concentrated on the ritual of *'ensabanado Fantomas,'* of rolling the joint. Morena honored me by offering it first to me. I joyfully inhaled twice and passed it over to Genovesa. The joint traveled from mouth to mouth as if we all were old comrades.

Right away, we slowed down our words; I got up to get the drinks before the usual laziness hit me. As I passed around the tray, I invited everyone to serve themselves the next rounds. Morena and Genovesa exchanged glances I didn't understand.

I wanted them to listen to a record of Alain Barriére. Genovesa said that the music reminded her of *el murmullo del mar,* the sounds of the sea. I lowered my voice down to a whisper, forcing them to close the circle around me.

"The tide," she said, placing her hand on my arm, "is like a dream." She longed to live near the ocean. "Perhaps like you," she said, her hand still on my arm. Her amber eyes attracted me and I feared her ex-husband would notice something.

"I'm not used to being touched," I told her quietly.

She gave me a startled look and pulled her hand away.

"When I was a child, my mother wouldn't let anybody touch me. She claimed I was allergic to human touch. Can you imagine?"

"Allergic? What do you mean?" she asked, moving away from me.

I regretted it immensely; a few more inches separated us now. I must win back what I have just so stupidly lost, I said to myself.

Raúl was drinking fast and I noticed the cousins were getting anxious. Genovesa said something to him about his liver, then quietly added that she didn't plan to take care of him tonight. "You'll be out in the cold this time," she whispered.

Uy, she's hard, I thought.

She wouldn't let the matter drop and it was impossible to keep a conversation going. "It seems useless to try to change him at this time of night," I said.

Raúl brightened; kneading circles on the rug with a giddy finger he told Genovesa she was still his muse. The muse bolted up like a wild animal.

"Muse, oh please. What you need is someone to rescue you from your drinking bouts."

I noticed there were tears in her eyes. I felt like hugging her and saying she shouldn't feel that bad. Morena had told me they were trying to stay friendly now that they had finally divorced. "Poor guys," she had said.

Raúl insisted as though he hadn't heard a word. He said how much he liked her Semitic woman's body. The subject was getting interesting, I thought, but then a black hole opened up and we all fell in.

Raúl decided to get up and take some fresh air; he stumbled across the living room. Morena and I giggled as he reached the carrousel with shaky steps. He looked at it with a childish expression and turned to ask me if he could climb on it.

"That's what they're for; they've been waiting all night," I answered.

15

I tried to get to my feet in order to turn the switch on, tripped on the scattered cushions and tumbled to the floor. My *femme fatale* character went down the drain. Both cousins rushed over to help me. Morena held her hand out and Genovesa took my arm; between the two they hauled me up. They were laughing wildly so I laughed too.

Raúl asked Morena to climb on the carrousel with him. She went back to the fireplace, let go of her bag for the first time and said no. Raúl insisted; he begged her to go soaring with him up into a cloud. When Genovesa urged her too, Morena got up *ipso facto*. Wow! the older cousin has power over the younger, I thought.

Morena studied the horses out of the corner of her eye. She chose the white *percheron,* that had its front legs lifted near its chest. Now that the others had moved to the opposite side of the room, Genovesa returned to the mirrors.

"Do you live here alone?" she asked.

"My sons live on the other side."

She was surprised to learn I had children. She wanted to know how old they were. "Eighteen and nineteen," I replied. She was even more surprised. "Yes and I'm about to be thirty-nine...that old."

"You don't look your age at all," she said, and after a pause, "I would like to be your age."

She said she was twenty-five.

Just then Raúl raised his voice. He claimed he was up in a cloud looking down on a woman they obviously all knew. I was struck by the way he spontaneously invented a hot story about her and a certain European prince.

Her name was Roberta and she was an actress. That's all I understood.

The prince's story was obviously aimed at Genovesa but it didn't appear to interest her at all. On the contrary, she seemed lost in her own thoughts.

Morena, anxious for her cousin, invited her to climb on the third horse. Genovesa prompted me to climb up instead. I went over, took her by the arm and told her that Mahoma, my favorite, would be delighted to ride with her. "He knows some magical places," I added.

"Mmmm, it's tempting," she said finally.

I helped her up onto the fierce grinning stallion. I noticed she tightened the grip of her thighs on the horse's belly as it moved up and down. Her shirt rose and fell with the breeze that drifted through the open window. She laughed; I thought she had a delicious way of laughing.

Just then, the door next to the fireplace flew open. Alberto, my son, walked quickly in and looked at my guests from head to toe. I introduced them; he hardly answered back. His arrogance got on my nerves, but I decided to simply invite him in. "Have a drink with us," I said.

He wouldn't accept. He just turned and walked out, slamming the door.

My three guests got down from the carrousel. Genovesa was pale with rage; she questioned my son's right to judge his mother's friends. I argued that it had been I who had invested him with that right after my divorce.

"Why do you always have to take sides with them?" Morena asked angrily.

We went to sit in front of the fireplace again but our spirits had cooled down; we were gloomy now. We spoke about the relationship between mother and child. They, having never been parents, had a different viewpoint from mine.

We said goodbye as the sun was coming up. To my surprise, I cried painfully when I went to bed. I felt sorry for myself. I couldn't be free, not even for one night; my own children wouldn't let me. I had passed on to them the rigid standards from which I now wanted to be free. I realized that I had helped to make my own prison.

FAREWELL TO
THE GOOD TIMES

I was standing in front of a tall iron gate in Barrilaco, one of México City's wealthiest districts. The cold was seeping into my bones and no one came to the door. After I had rung several times, an elderly woman finally appeared. She was wearing huge glasses which were perched on her little nose.

I asked for Morena. She looked me over from head to toe and said, "Come in."

We walked across the garden in silence. There was a fragrant smell of freshly cut grass. Once inside, she pointed to a red-carpeted wooden stair. 'Upstairs', she signaled, and disappeared through the jamb of a double door that probably led to the kitchen.

Climbing up the stairs, I looked at everything around me through my sociologist's eye and concluded it was the home of *nouveau riche* proprietors. Ah! a lofty lady's portrait hung on the wall. It must be Genovesa's mother, I thought. It was strange, I always used to think of the cousins as sisters and now, in the house where they both grew up, this made an impact on me.

As I stood there, Morena came out of a room and looked at me in wonder.

"You weren't coming, right?" she asked, glancing at her watch. I didn't know what to say.

She led me into the bedroom that she and Genovesa had shared when they were children. A thick layer of smoke screened the bodies that were scattered on the floor. I imagined chameleons resting on top of steaming rocks.

Everybody turned to gaze at me when Morena introduced me as her friend Valeria. Genovesa came over to say hello. I looked for a sign of recognition in her face but couldn't find any. From that moment on, she gave herself to the task of hostess. I sat on the sofa she had left vacant next to the window and cursed myself for having wanted to see her again so badly.

I took off my tweed jacket, folded up my shirt sleeves; my boots gleamed under the lamp light. I felt as distant as a lonely star. I watched the chameleons through the big mirror on the closet door. Genovesa came back with the drinks. I was the last to receive my glass of red wine. She smiled gently.

"You don't drink anything else, right?"

"I'm a woman of set tastes," I answered.

She looked tired and sad. Life isn't easy for the young either, I thought. She walked towards a blue-eyed woman sitting on the bed. Raúl moved his African queen-style chair back to let them be alone. Somebody whispered that she was the famous Roberta. By her looks, I guessed she was an actress and a daughter of wealthy parents. Our eyes met and, without any ostensible reason, we declared war on each other.

Sitting next to me was a man with straight black hair who looked Chinese. When I heard his name was David, I recalled Morena saying he was a good poet and a friend of hers. He was chatting with Marta, the well-known Mexican feminist, about mass media's noxious effects on our social system. "Have you noticed that every spokesperson in Televisa always shares the government's views?" she asked. "It's a disgrace, don't you think?"

I thought of joining in the conversation but I didn't feel like talking.

A new round of drinks arrived. "Uf, perfect timing," I murmured. David turned around to look at me. "Life's not easy," I said. He agreed. After a few more sips, I felt the tension in my muscles slacken.

I watched Genovesa talking with Roberta. All of a sudden, she hit the mattress with her fist. She turned to see if anyone had noticed; no, luckily not, she thought.

For no reason, I recalled the three bleeding bulls' heads on the plaza in Janitzio and felt like throwing up again. Morena came over to ask me if I was feeling all right. I was amazed that it all showed in my face.

I told her I didn't know what it would be like after she'd gone. Tears welled up in her eyes and she begged me not to talk about her departure.

"It's time to go, then," I said, letting down my shirt sleeves, when a young man with an androgynous look walked into the room. His nose was very crooked.

He said he was sorry he was so late, but he had been at a play reading of a dear friend and couldn't leave any earlier. He looked around carefully before deciding where to sit and then picked a place next to mine. He introduced himself; his name was Janosh and he was of Hungarian descent. He said he had seen me in the Colegio de México but his face didn't seem familiar. I told him I was about to leave when he came in.

"Really? Why don't you stay a while longer?"

Before I knew it, we were getting drunk and drifting in happy conversation. He confessed he was very nervous and excited because he was leaving for Bangladesh in a few hours.

"In search of the light," he added.

"I just read some grafitti in the San Miguel Chapultepec district that said, 'Bangladesh, where the best rock & roll is played!' Can you believe it?"

He laughed sourly. "I saw that too, near Genovesa's place, right?" and added gloomily, "If only that were the whole truth."

"Yes," I replied, taking note of where the lady lived; the lady who didn't seem to be interested in me, I reminded myself.

Just then, Genovesa surprised me by coming to sit at my feet. She tried to talk to me but I felt it was too late for that. She had taken much too long. So she and Janosh started a conversation. I learned that he was leaving on the same plane as Morena and he would be making his connection to India from Paris. I imagined him and Morena sitting next to each other on the plane, Janosh with his mystical face, she with her silver paper collars hanging from her neck. Two sad people saying goodbye to this cruel México.

I told myself that if I didn't talk with Genovesa I would later regret it. But I was still furious and couldn't break my coldness.

"This time I'm leaving."

Morena came over to hug me and reminded me of our agreement.

"Goodbye everybody," I mumbled, waving my hand.

Genovesa offered to come out with me to the car. I said it was not necessary, but luckily she insisted. We walked downstairs in silence.

Looking at the woman with the amber eyes, I switched on the engine and stepped on the gas like a rebellious adolescent.

As I sped away, I watched her through the rear view mirror as she grew smaller and smaller.

BAD PREMONITIONS

As dawn approached, I heard the sound of voices singing in a nearby garden; death songs. Perhaps Morena was in danger. I had to tell someone and her cousin was the only person who would listen.

My wish grew stronger as the days went on, but judging from my dramatic exit the other night I had the feeling it was dangerous to go near her. When I finally dialed her number my hand was shaking.

She answered, saying she had also been tempted to call. Morena had left her a note with my phone number asking her to call me.

"And why didn't you?" I asked, "I would've been very happy."

"After the other night," she confessed, "I was afraid to."

I had never expected such an answer and it took me off guard. Now I would hear the other side of the story.

We agreed to meet and I went to pick her up. I parked in front of her studio. After I heard the six electronic bells of the nearby church, I rang the buzzer. Genovesa stuck her head out of the window and yelled that she was coming down.

When I saw her walking out the glass door of the old building, my heart leapt. She walked gracefully, holding her head high. She was wearing a dark skirt and a magenta blouse. She looked like a gypsy.

She climbed into the car and said hello with a kiss that barely touched my cheek. Then she looked fixedly at me. "Which of the two women are you?" she asked earnestly. "The one I met the first night or the other, the second night?"

"Both," I said, much against my will. "The one who lets me fully enjoy life and the other one who forbids me to." She smiled as if she understood perfectly.

I suggested we go for drinks somewhere she liked. She thought it over a minute and then ceremoniously said, "Go ahead." She sat comfortably back in her seat and guided me to the lakeside on the new Chapultepec.

The head waiter showed us to a window table. Two black clouds, slim as daggers, slit the red sky. Genovesa asked for a whiskey and I ordered a bottle of *Siglo*. The fountain in the middle of the lake spurted a powerful stream that sprayed the windows with a light mist.

I confessed that the reason I was in a bad mood the other night was because I had been badly wanting to see her.

"Bad mood? You seemed furious," she interrupted. "I had been thinking about you too," she said. "But I've been going through a crisis, you know?"

"Raúl?"

"No, not just him."

The drinks arrived and we toasted, looking into each other's eyes.

"Roberta, you remember who she is?" she asked. "When she came back from Paris, where she had been studying, she didn't want to go back to her parents' house, so I invited her to share my apartment. Raúl and I were just getting separated and he was about to move out."

A long silence ensued as she took a few drags of her cigarette.

"Now she's moving out too," she added. "All of my friends who had sworn everlasting friendship are not here to comfort me now that I need them." A look of pain came to her face.

I kept wondering who Roberta was. Was she a dear friend, a passionate lover? I was dying to ask, but I didn't dare; I figured it was wiser to wait.

"All relationships erode with time," she said sadly. "None of them last."

"Not always," I assured her. "A few passionate encounters turn out to be *buenos amores*, good love relationships."

"Do you really believe that?"

"I'm positive."

She laughed and asked if I myself had found a good love yet. "No, unfortunately not," I said. "But I'm sure it won't be long now."

"I can't decide if you're an optimist or an incurable romantic," she said and we laughed.

She asked if I now understood why she hadn't been friendlier that night. Yes, I nodded. But I didn't tell her that the mechanism of my anger had blinded me, my lack of understanding taking over like a dead weight.

Now that the conversation was starting to warm up, I decided to ask, "And who's Roberta, besides being your roommate?"

She said Roberta had translated a play which she was directing and had invited Genovesa to work on. "The Transvestite Prince" was a comedy by the eighteenth-century French writer Marivaux. She would sit in the first row every night, watching rehearsals.

"Nobody knew who I was," she said, smiling. "I was the stage director but I was Roberta's advisor too. This we had to keep a secret."

"But why was it a secret?" I wanted to know. She was very quiet and I noticed there were tears in her eyes.

"Let's talk about something else—you don't mind, do you?"

She soon regained her composure and asked me to tell her about myself. She was curious to know about my marriage.

"Did you love him?" she asked.

The question surprised me. I hadn't thought about it in such a long time.

"No, I was never in love with him," I said finally. "Nor was he in love with me. He married me for my father's money; he confessed it right away," I added. "Years later, at the end of my psychoanalysis, I had to admit that I had married without being in love. The first few years I hated him but, as time went on, we settled into a quiet relationship. We had two sons: that's what was important to me."

"I can't believe someone like you would spend thirteen years with a husband you didn't love."

"My children were small. I didn't want them to live without a father."

She argued that she still couldn't understand. "Children never appreciate that sort of thing," she claimed.

The waiter came over to ask if we wanted anything else. Genovesa ordered a cognac. When the waiter left she asked suddenly, "And have you ever been in love?"

I told her my story with Arturo, the one man I had fallen deeply in love with but whom my parents wouldn't let me marry.

"Why wouldn't they let you?"

"My parents thought he wasn't worthy of me. Besides, my father has always been a puritan and the family name has been his main concern. When he found out that Arturo's mother had a lover, he forbade me to see him again. Arturo proposed that we escape together and get married, but I was too young and didn't dare to," I recalled with bitterness.

"I was in love with him all through my marriage. Then, ten years later, I accidentally ran into him and realized, for the first time, that he was a total stranger."

I seized the moment to tell her that I had been recently proposed to by Alejandro and was considering getting married again.

"Would you marry again?"

It was obvious from her face that my image had shattered before her eyes. Her doubt was so strong it hit me.

"He's the first man that both my children and my parents like since my divorce six years ago." I didn't want to mention that I wanted to get married before turning forty because men wouldn't like me after that. She made no further comments and I glanced at her watch.

I had made an evening appointment with Alejandro. I didn't feel like leaving her now that the evening was just starting, so I asked her if she wanted to spend some more time with an interesting woman.

"Meaning yourself? Well, you're modest," she laughed.

She argued that it was too late to cancel my appointment but I said it was just a matter of getting through a bad moment.

The phone at the restaurant was out of order so I called Alejandro, my future husband, from a pay phone in Reforma. It was right in front of the bus stop; he couldn't hear a word. I repeated that I was at an important meeting and couldn't leave.

"You can chat with your friend some other time," he said, furious. "You come right away, you hear? I'm waiting for you at my house."

"Time is almost up and I don't have any more coins," I countered and hung up the receiver. I was elated: I was a free woman now. Genovesa chuckled in complicity as I climbed back into the car. We headed south.

SOUTH

We had both always lived at the other end of the city and this trip meant we were leaving behind our pasts.

We were looking for a place that would give us shelter. I recalled a charming little restaurant where we could keep on talking about ourselves.

We walked down the spiral stairs into a small bar furnished in dark woods, imitation English style.

It was early and we found a small table in the corner where we could feel isolated from the rest of the world. I asked for a tequila Conmemorativo and Genovesa went on drinking cognac.

I was curious to know about Roberta, what she meant in Genovesa's life. I had to find a means to bring up the subject, so I tried telling her a story from my past—the story of Ada.

The beautiful Ada was an Australian woman born in Poland whom I had met on Ischia, a little Italian island in the Mediterranean were I used to spend summers with my parents after my divorce.

"This woman," I told Genovesa, "was Jewish and had incomparable sea-green eyes. She was married to an English lord, and once a year they would go separate ways so she could rest from their active social life.

"One evening I saw her standing between the golden vines that framed the main door to the restaurant of the Regina Margherita. She was waiting for the maitre d' to escort her to her table.

"I noticed how he rushed to receive her bowing deeply, and led her with ill-concealed pleasure into the dining room. She walked across the floor dressed in a long gown, jeweled to perfection. The clatter of silverware ceased until the woman sat in her assigned place.

27

"The guests always had fixed tables during their stay," I said, pausing. Genovesa had lit another cigarette and seemed to be enjoying the story.

"One night, Ada looked over to our table at the blue Tibetan tea box my mother always brought with her. 'Such a beautiful container,' she exclaimed in her English accent.

"'Would you like to try some of the tea?' I asked promptly.

"'Oh, I would be delighted,' she answered.

"I suggested an after-dinner tea and she readily accepted, so I patiently waited until tea-time.

"Before we had even sat down, I proposed we have a drink instead of tea. 'At the hotel bar on the terrace,' I said.

"'Better yet, why don't we go out?' she countered. 'To the Regina discoteque, for instance.'

"Her proposal surprised me, but I loved the idea of leaving those musty surroundings for a while."

"Was she beautiful?" Genovesa interrupted with a flicker in her eyes.

"Very beautiful."

"And how old was she?"

"Forty-five," I answered, and noticed her puzzled look. "Why? Do you think that's too old?"

"No. I just thought she was younger than you. Don't mistake me, I like women your age," she said, looking down at her drink and then into my eyes. "But, tell me, did you dance with her?"

"Dancing was not her *forte,* so we sat at a table and I looked closely into those green eyes.

"Ada and I talked a lot that night. At one point, we started speaking about infidelity. It was then that she told me of a small hill town on Capri that had just a few tiny white houses. She said it was an ideal place for lovers to go and prompted me to visit it someday. 'I would love to see such a paradise,' I told her."

"And did you?" Genovesa asked, pulling her chair closer to hear my reply.

I didn't answer. Her curiosity emboldened me to ask about Roberta. There was a pause.

"What do you want to know?" she asked.

"Was she your lover?"

She kept quiet and puffed out rings of smoke up to the ceiling.

"You're daring," she said. "And you? Did you and Ada go to the hill of the white houses?"

"Mmmm," I mumbled with my eyes fixed on her lips. I felt such strong desire for her that I decided not to fight against it.

"Did you go?" she insisted, putting her hand on my forearm. "Whoops! I'm sorry," she said, for having touched me.

I told her she could touch me as much as she wanted. I said this, brushing my finger over the golden down on her arm. She answered by holding my finger.

The world vanished for a moment.

Then a loud street fight began. We were surrounded in a second by intermittent lights and the noise of sirens. We heard a gunshot and the voices rose to yells. We paid and rushed out.

The man working in the parking lot said they had found a distinguished gentleman lying dead in the street around the corner.

Only then did we notice it was morning, and we still had so much to tell each other.

For once I decided not to put my children first. Instead of rushing home immediately, I invited her for an early breakfast at El Moro downtown. *Churros* and chocolate were a good way to start a day like this. Over our steaming cups, I finally brought up the subject of Morena. She was after all the person who had brought this woman and me together.

Genovesa was quiet for a long time; unexpected gloom seemed to hang over her.

"I fear for her life," she said at last. "I hope she's strong enough to make it."

I saw that it was too harsh a subject to bring up just then so I dropped it entirely.

A few minutes later, sipping our chocolate *a la francesa,* she turned her eyes to me and we were right back where we had been hotly hovering the whole night.

It was noon when I took her to her house.

I waited until she disappeared through the glass door of her old building. I longed for her immediately. I turned away in my black Mustafá with a sudden rush of fear. Perhaps I wouldn't see her again.

29

WOODEN FLOORS

She had told me she lived in a fourth-floor apartment and there was no elevator. I climbed as swiftly as a sea gull flies. She was leaning against the open door, waiting. I noticed she looked very much like me; the impression made my heart pound fast. She asked if anything was wrong. "No, everything's fine," I said, and she smiled, inviting me in.

I entered a huge room with worn-out wooden floors. The emptiness appalled me and I felt a chill. I didn't know if it came from the outside or from inside me. I hugged myself.

She noticed my bewilderment. "Is it different from what you expected?" she asked.

"Yes, quite different," I replied, and she laughed at my frankness.

At the far end of the studio an unfinished canvas stood on an easel. It was a picture of a window that looked onto a cold sea. "It's like a dream turned real," I remarked. She said the image came out of her longing for the ocean.

There were two tall stools standing near the easel. She offered me the highest. With her painting as a backdrop, it all seemed like a stage set. I wondered if I was expected to show a talent for acting. As if she had read my mind, she added that our places were interchangeable.

When we sat down, I noticed, facing us, a brass mirror that framed our heads. In its reflection the ocean of her painting served as a background. The place I occupied was the vanishing point where all angles met.

As I pondered this, she suddenly remembered something she had in the kitchen. I was left to scrutinize her apartment with eyes accustomed to my own baroque spaces. The Fallen Countess came back with a delicious gift: *Siglo,* my favorite wine. She poured it into two glasses and handed me one. My eyes flowed between her mouth and the red liquid. She lifted her copper-colored hair, letting her neck show, and looked at herself in the mirror. I felt such a rush of desire for this stranger that my eyes nearly flooded.

Pink Floyd was somewhere in the background, adrift on an old record player. She said the phonograph had belonged to her grandfather, whom she tenderly called Bear. Bear used to give her big hugs and kisses when she visited him in his workshop. She described his tough hands working on the delicate machinery of old clocks. I liked the feel of her roots.

Hanging from one of the white walls were three photographs of women. I wanted to know who they were. The woman in the long peasant dress and loose chignon was her grandmother's mother. She held a pretty little girl on her lap, Genovesa's grandmother. They were sitting under the shade of a willow tree in their Russian home town before the First World War. In another picture, a young woman in a strapless black dress stood aloof in the midst of a crowd.

"That's my mother in the fifties, right after I was born....And that's my grandmother again, sitting next to Bear." Genovesa pointed to the third one.

Beautiful and distinguished, the three women had something distant in their gaze. Each of them wore the same cameo, one that Genovesa said had belonged in the family for many generations.

"How surprising to see the same jewel passing from hand to hand without being lost," I remarked.

Genovesa, with a charming gesture, touched the cameo now pinned to the breast of her gold-embroidered black blouse. I moved closer to her to get a better look. I whispered that it was very beautiful, but with the excuse of serving more wine, she cut my remarks short.

"That's why you're so attractive," I added, looking at the women she came from. I took a sip of the *Siglo*.

Suddenly, I noticed a small bedside table standing near the entrance door as if it were leaving at any moment. That small piece of furniture helped me step into my hostess' life.

She had followed my gaze. "Roberta just moved away," she said. "The moving van was full, so she had to leave that behind."

She swept her eyes across the studio and sighed. I wondered if she was thinking about how little she owned. She confessed she would have a lot of free time now: time to paint, to read, to walk around the city. Ah, but above all, she said, she would never fall in love again. "I don't believe in love anymore," she claimed sadly.

"You mean Roberta?"

"No, I mean in general."

My eyes lingered on her mouth. She left the stool nervously and went to stand by the window, where she stared at something only she could see. My gaze drifted back to her sea and my desire stirred violently. She turned around and seemed surprised to find me there. To hide the fact, she invited me to stand with her. She pointed out the window to the right. Surrounded by a formless amber cloud, the Castillo de Chapultepec stood majestically on the hilltop. The last rays of sun filtered through her hair, turning it an even deeper copper. My naughty hand obeyed an unconscious command and caressed it. Genovesa turned toward me with a puzzled look. I apologized, only half sorry. She was taking my hand as if to slap it when the bell rang. We were both startled. "Who can it be? I'm not expecting anybody," she said, glancing at her watch. She threw the window open and yelled out. A man's voice answered back. Happy, she asked him to come up. Bad luck, I thought.

A redhead with ragged pants came into the studio. When he saw me standing there, he excused himself and told Genovesa he hadn't thought to ask if she had visitors. He was just back from the movie studio where he was editing the film he had finished shooting. He was exhilarated and began to talk passionately about his work. The tension disappeared as we discovered that we both shared a love for acting. Soon, he and I were standing in the middle of the floor, improvising an erotic scene before our hostess' sharp eye. I did a sketch we named 'The quiet step of a violet lady.' It was a monologue that ended in tragic murder. There was such a flow of creativity that before I noticed it was four in the morning.

"My children will be worried." I was dismayed.

"It's too late for you to drive back alone," Erick said. I agreed, but I had never failed to return home. Genovesa declared that she wouldn't let me go at such an hour.

"You'll call them in the morning," she advised.

I had to confess to myself I didn't feel like leaving the two of them alone together, but there was a little problem: there was only her bed and a mattress on the floor of the empty room.

A flip of the coin settled who would share Genovesa's bed and I won it.

After we finally got into bed, I had all my thoughts placed on her body; how to touch her. When I made up my mind and slipped my arm around her appealing waist, she quietly moved it away.

"It's better if we get some sleep," she whispered.

Neither of us slept a wink.

SO DISCIPLINED

"Nothing, not even a raucous nightlife, should be a reason to fail my obligations," I scolded myself. I made use of my well-honed discipline and left for the university. Sitting in front of Professor Hugo—Argentinian, neurotic and loquacious—my mind started roaming. I remembered he liked bourgeois women. "They wear perfume, they visit the hairdresser regularly and, above all, they have learned the laws of seduction and love," he used to tell me. How come good old Hugo, with all his knowledge, had problems with his erection? His explanation was simple: he had a domineering mother. Using that confession as evidence and taking a closer inspection of the subject, I built my own theory: acute misogyny.

My classmates' arguments on Marx's theory of exploitation seemed endless, and Genovesa's face kept popping up from an ivory cornucopia. I wished I could be sailing the torrents of her released emotions, so distant from Hugo's rhetorical language. It was then and there that I realized the absurdity of academic life. Before I knew it, I was standing by the door telling Hugo, "Goodbye, I have urgent matters to attend to, goodbye."

I wanted to go to Genovesa's house, but I didn't dare arrive unannounced. I didn't feel like going back to mine either. Restless, I decided to take a stroll in Chapultepec Park; that was the nearest to her I could be. Walking on the paths through the trees, I had a sudden awareness of the many roads I had taken in my life.

Each time I started on a new adventure, I plunged into it feeling it was of utmost importance. I never looked back. My Scorpio moon constantly urged me to find something new. The present moment was born with a bang, and all that existed before died irrevocably away.

I lay down in the shade of a tree, felt the waves of exhaustion reach me and entered a long tunnel. It was dream's silent space.

When I woke up I drove home. I went through the garden and climbed the lovers' staircase so no one would see me. I closed the heavy curtains of my bedroom windows and fell asleep the moment I laid my head on the pillow. When I awoke I found out my sons had gone out.

"Good!" I said to myself, "now it's my turn to live." I jumped out of bed in a hurry.

Erick was throwing a masquerade party. It was *Día de Muertos* and my new acquaintance had invited me to the celebration. Naturally, I had no costume to wear because I had preferred to sleep. This nonsense made me anxious so I decided I would wear my everyday disguise.

I dressed in front of the mirror. I slipped into my tight jeans, put on a pair of lustrous cowboy boots with raven-beak heels, tilted my felt hat with its quail feather at just the right angle. I took three steps back and looked at myself.

"Not bad," I said to my reflection.

PUENTE DE MUERTOS

I was surrounded by skeletons, by men dressed as women, women dressed as men. Everything was enveloped in a veil of cigarette smoke. The penetrating smell of makeup filled the air. The music was a strident rock, probably played by some German band.

I walked, click, clack, following scraps of conversation; the trivia was crazy.

"Me...very happy!"

I turned to see who the lucky guy was. Uy! he had mice teeth. "And how are you?" he asked.

"Me?...just waiting for someone," I answered.

"Stood up?"

"That's possible."

We started to talk. He said he was a skin repairer. "Snake or crocodile skin?" I asked.

"Human," he said. "I work at the morgue," and he motioned with his hand as if ripping flesh with a scalpel.

I remembered Rembrandt's famous painting of a doctor and his pupils, all dressed in black, gathered around an open corpse.

Suddenly there was a surge in the electric current, the lights went out and the entrance door flew open as if impelled by the wind. She walked in, dressed in black, a mushroom-shaped hat on her head. Half of her face smiled and the other half was stained with tears. A small red moon in decline shone over the smiling half. Marvelous! I thought.

"That's her," I told the mortician.

"Whoa!" He was shocked.

The woman came in without looking at anyone. She stopped to listen to the music; keeping time with her head, she started dancing to "Let It Be." I was aware of the difference between our rhythms; I liked hers. She swept the floor with her eyes, found me and came over. I asked her to dance with me. She gave me a puzzled look. "Yes," she said, moving with her drum cadence. Mine was winds. I took her by the waist and matched our rhythms. She let her eyes drop abruptly.

"To couple, that's the secret," I whispered softly in her ear.

I felt a desire to kiss her. Right then Erick appeared on the dance floor; the three of us danced together. He, getting hot, proposed we make love. I was about to say I didn't like sharing when somebody touched his arm: he had a phone call from L.A.

Genovesa took this opportunity to tell me, "I'm going to the ocean tomorrow. I need to put the latest events of my life in order."

She had bought her plane ticket a week ago. The news struck me dumb. I wanted to know if I would be included in this sorting out.

"Perhaps," she said, thinking it over.

"I'll be away for the holiday also; I invited Alejandro to my house in San Miguel."

"Will you marry him?"

"Do you really want to know?"

She wavered for a moment. "Yes, I do."

"I want to give myself the chance to find out. He might persuade me."

I could see she disliked my answer but made no comment.

"It's a pity," I said, brushing her neck with my mouth. She stepped back.

"What's a pity?" I stroked the happy half of her face. She stopped my hand. "For someone who's afraid to be touched, you touch a lot," she said.

I walked her to her car.

"Yes," she said, "it's a pity," and left.

THE TWISTS OF FATE

I was sound asleep when I heard the phone ringing in the distance. It was Alejandro's daughter. Her father was in the hospital, probably from a heart attack. I was dumbfounded. A heart attack? I told her I wouldn't be long, hung up and fell back to sleep. A few moments later I woke up with a start, made myself a cup of strong black coffee, showered and got dressed. I remembered that poor Alex had told me he didn't know how to enjoy life. He'd said he'd love me to show him how: through my love of literature, music, good wines, travel, and the sea. He hadn't had time to explore the good things in life because he had been working nonstop. Now he had lots of money and didn't know how to spend it.

Before I was aware of it, I was parking in front of the Hospital Inglés.

I had arranged to meet Adela next to the information desk, but she wasn't there. Damn! All that effort to rush over and show my concern went down the drain.

Just then, Adela came out of the elevator, in the middle of a huge yawn. I imagined the tonsils in her throat. I asked if her father was better.

"Better, why should he be better?" she said, ill-tempered.

"You're right, *pendeja*."

On the third floor a huge-breasted nurse came out of Alejandro's room. Suddenly, the simple idea of spending a whole day in the hospital was the worst thing I could imagine.

When I entered the room his brother was already there. Alejandro had a catheter stuck to his arm and was pale as death. But as soon as he saw me, he wanted me to tell his brother how he had predicted something would happen to him before our trip.

"Trip?" I asked.

38

"Yes, our trip to San Miguel," he said. "Didn't I tell you something would happen?"

"Yes, you mentioned it a few days ago." I smiled.

Having settled that, he motioned with his finger for me to come sit at his side. I hated the idea but I climbed up on the bed with an agile little jump. While I was stroking his head, Adela sat on the sofa by the window, putting on the last touches of her makeup.

"Look at her," her father said, "just like a clown. When will you show her how to do it? Watch Valeria, can't you see how attractive she makes herself?"

I felt sorry for the teenager and told her I thought she put it on better than I did. Just then, Alejandro's married daughter rushed in to see her father. She was red-faced from running and her voice was unbearably high-pitched.

"Didn't I tell you?" she asked her father.

"What did you tell me?" he answered, mimicking her.

"That you're no longer young enough to go out carousing every night. Eh, didn't I tell you? Yes or no?" she pressed on, staring at me.

"But he's not an old man either," I interrupted. "I go to bed late myself and look, nothing's wrong with me."

"Please, Valeria, don't compare yourself with my father, will you. He has suffered too much."

Surely they must own the patent for suffering, I thought. That's what I get for meddling.

It wasn't long before the procession of distressed friends arrived. The first to come in were a strange couple. Alejandro introduced me as his fiancée.

"Are you Don Marcelo's daughter?" the woman asked.

"That's right!" Alejandro answered conceitedly.

The husband, wearing a second-class toupee, stared. "Yes, yes, oh yes. It's a pleasure, a real pleasure."

The nurse saved the situation; she had come back to examine the patient. "I have to check him all over," she said with a horny smile. "Please, everyone out." I couldn't help noticing a look of complicity between Alejandro and his brother.

Outside in the hallway, the world came back to my senses. Hospitals depressed me; I couldn't stop thinking about death. I went down to the basement for a cup of coffee.

When I came back to the room, Ema the nurse said Alejandro had been asking for us. He was flushed with excitement. He told me that he was in perfect health, his heart was back to normal. We could go to San Miguel right away. He said this last with a loving look in his eyes. I got goose pimples. The nurse interrupted us, suggesting he should wait until tomorrow when the resident doctor could do a final examination and release him.

"That's a definite no," he said. "My honeymoon can't wait."

I said quickly that we could go away the following week. The sugary expression on his face turned into a mask of hate.

"You want to make me feel like a cripple?" He finished the phrase with a viperish whistle. "Answer me!"

I saw myself married to him, his entire family surrounding us. The picture made me shiver.

The married daughter, not interested in the outcome of our life story, said she had to leave. She was already late picking up her little girl at her mother's house.

"I'm coming with you," I said.

"That's impossible," Alejandro protested. "We haven't had time to be alone together."

My decision was made. Snapping my fingers, I said goodbye to everyone.

"*No, no, no, no señor,* I'll never marry you, tirutita, taratata," I sang to myself.

I left the hospital in high gear. I needed a hot bath to wash away the bad spirits.

Agustín, my housekeeper, had left a note on the bed: 'Genovesa called, she is in the city.' My heart leapt. Agustín must have made a mistake, I thought as I dialed her number.

"*Los muy cabrones* at Mexicana overbooked the flight and ten of us had to stay back. Can you believe it?"

Her rage made me giggle. It was the best news I had received in years but I told her it was a real pity. She didn't believe me. She wanted to know how come I was in the city too. I told her what had happened to Alejandro, and we had a good laugh. I was beginning to believe that all of this was a twist of fate. It seemed incredible that we were both in México. Now I wanted to learn the meaning of it all....

I changed clothes and rushed over to visit her. We stayed up talking until dawn.

40

The next day the phone woke me up again. I answered rudely: why didn't they ever let me sleep? Genovesa, hearing my tone of voice, told me I should call her back when I was fully awake and hung up. I called her back immediately.

"I thought it was Alejandro," I said.

"So that's how you treat your future husband?"

"*No, no, no, no señor,* I'll never marry you," I sang, and we both laughed.

I wanted to invite her to spend *Puente de Muertos* at my house. The children had gone with my parents to L.A. and the servants had asked my permission to return to their home towns. She said it seemed crazy. She, in my house with me.

I plotted with care to convince her it wasn't crazy. Little by little my strategy seemed to be winning her over, but her fears were not metaphorical. I'm not sure how I reached such flights of passion, but I promised her the ocean. The tone of my voice softened and I let my desire speak. Touché! Something I said moved her heart. She accepted, but first I had to promise I would let her leave any time she wanted to. I felt like Dangerous Valeria. I replied, with a hint of danger in my voice, that her wishes were my commands.

"I'll just change from my tropical clothes into something more suitable and I'll be right over," she said, her voice trembling slightly.

WAITING

In front of the mirror I drew a thin black line on each of my eyelids: a subtle frame. "Ommmm," I repeated until I had a tickling sensation on the edges of my lips. "Why did you invite her home?" I asked myself, feeling a spur of adrenalin shoot through my body.

I slipped into my tight jeans and put on a blood-colored silk shirt. Swish, swosh! I swept my belt across my butt. I was a woman of stubborn habits, why had I invited a stranger to my house? Well, well...I put 'red-earth' blush on my cheeks. "My fears are not metaphorical, either," I said to myself. I dismissed the thought with a gesture of my hand, fixed my aura of impeccable persona and walked out on stage. I designed the lights and shadows, giving it all a casual look. I leaned out of the window and watched Agustín watering the plants in the garden. He always did this before leaving, otherwise his mind gave him no rest when he was away, he always said. I asked him to bring up all the roses he could find in the greenhouse.

"All of them?" he asked, puzzled.

I spread the Philippine shawl on top of the bed. Agustín came up with seven vases of colorful roses. I gave him a list of the things I would need for him to buy before he left. "A friend is coming over to stay with me," I told him.

"*Qué bueno,* so you won't be all alone."

Agustín had been working with me for the past thirteen years. He was just a child when he first arrived in the house. I was a child myself, but with two sons already.

"I'll be back soon," he smiled. I smiled back.

Suddenly I heard wings beating on the terrace. I rushed out, wondering if the birds had brought a message for me. The flock passed on and I was alone again.

42

I spent time stripping the withered leaves from the flower pots; I didn't know what else to do. Then I sat down and watched the trees swaying in the breeze. Time passed so slowly! I went in for a book but couldn't find a single one that attracted me. I finally picked up a novel by Goytisolo, but then I couldn't concentrate. "I'll just exchange a few things in my suitcase," she had said, "and I'll be right there. I expect it's going to be a great holiday."

This is the story of my life, I thought with rage, always waiting. It occurred to me that perhaps she was having her own dilemmas and I calmed down. Maybe she's asking herself why she agreed to spend her holiday with an older woman.

I imagined her sitting next to the window looking out on the gray mass of buildings around her. Three, ten tons of cement underneath a rarified sky. She could at least call to say she'll be late, I thought. Perhaps she's not even coming. Damn it! I shut my eyes. A striped furry kitten appeared under my eyelids. It had a small head and eyes like emeralds. It wore a red chain around its neck. The chain turned into a serpent; the serpent slid smoothly towards me. I jumped out of the chair and went to look down on the street. Genovesa was nowhere to be seen.

I'm going to call her and tell her not to come anymore. But my eyes were glued to the asphalt strip. A tear came sliding down my cheek. Suddenly I noticed her ramshackle VW Bug turning the corner. She stepped out of the car, a brown overnight bag swinging from her shoulder. She looked around to make sure the world was still in place and split the pavement with her steady step.

Agustín arrived at that moment and switched open the electric door; their eyes met. The woman standing upstairs on the terrace hoarsely shouted an order: "Lock and chain." Genovesa looked up, held her hand over her eyes and smiled at me. She made her victorious entry into my world. I felt like applauding. I bent down to fix my hair and wiped away the remains of a furtive tear. I heard the strong tapping of her heels on the stairs.

VICTORIOUS ENTRY

Her boot heels clicked on the steps. She dropped her brown night bag on the red brick floor of the terrace, fixed her eyes on mine and asked if this were a kidnapping. It hadn't occurred to me, to tell the truth, but it was a sensational idea. Anyway, I preferred to make her responsible, so I told her that she had to be aware of her role as accomplice.

She considered this for a moment but didn't seem quite convinced. Then she brought out a bouquet of beautiful mexican lilies from behind her back. "They're for you," she said. I thanked her for her thoughtfulness and kissed her cheek. Then she pursued the matter again:

"And tell me, do you take pleasure in holding your guests as hostages?"

"Yes, it's very exciting," I claimed with just the shadow of a smile.

I felt like the heroine of a picture I hadn't seen yet—a film about to be shot; we would of course be the main characters. I said this and her eyes glowed like embers about to ignite.

We sat under the shade of the *jacaranda* tree. She lit a cigarette and left the pack on the wooden table. I noticed her hand was shaking. With her eyes she followed the trail of mold that ran from our table to the Oaxacan pots. I toasted to her arrival and asked what took her so long.

"Did I take too long? ... I had things to do."

Once again her feelings were so different from mine. She had taken so long only because she had things to do, not because she'd had doubts about coming. She never would have guessed that I had been desperately waiting. Now I felt sorry for having been so anxious and insecure.

Agustín came up to say goodbye. He took a careful look at my guest and smiled at her to show his approval. He wished us a good holiday and left. Once he had disappeared through the lovers' door, Genovesa asked if there was anybody else attending in the house.

"We're absolutely alone now," I said, pretending to scare her. She sipped her wine and took a long drag of her cigarette. I could sense she was looking at me with desire she couldn't control. I asked myself out loud if it could be possible that my guest was dangerous. My heart told me she was. "Perhaps," I said, "the risks of the game are equal for both."

She got up suddenly, as if propelled by a spring. She walked towards the cluster of lilacs that some dusky birds were pecking and stood there motionless, like a modern mannequin. I followed close behind her, my breath almost on her neck. She turned around. I noticed her conspicuous eyes, remarkably well painted.

The flowers on the terrace were flashing their bright colors. Alameda, my chihuahua dog, came running in, barking in her high-pitched voice. *La bella* smiled but did not pet the animal. She wanted to know why there were so many flowers blooming out of season.

"Who's responsible for this prodigy?"

"I'm the caretaker," I said with no humility.

"Is that how you take care of what you love?" she said glancing at me out of the corner of her eye.

"I have more of a problem with human beings."

"Do you? Nobody would have said so." She had the feeling I was such a *leve persona*, a light person. She walked to the table.

"Do you want something to eat?" I asked. She wasn't hungry.

"I'm hungry most of the day," I confessed and stood up to go prepare a food tray. I felt her eyes on me as I walked self-consciously into the bedroom.

I peeped out from the edge of the bedroom curtains and watched her. The way she looked at things was like a state of mind; a mood. Crish, crash: a hairy-legged spider came stumbling out of the curtain folds. I moved away.

A while later I came back out with a tray of delicious food. A scent of *zempasúchiles* reached my nose; dogs were howling in the distance.

We are all dying, I thought to myself.

Genovesa came to help me with the food. She inadvertently brushed my hand and pulled hers away immediately.

I poured the *Margaux Laffite* into two glasses. Little by little we ate scrumptiously.

There were endless tree-tops all the way to the horizon. The gray sky turned pink, then mauve.

I poured fresh wine into our glasses; the liquid came up to our lips. She wondered out loud how it would feel to be a prisoner like this. We toasted: I, for my prisoner, she, for her fantasy of days by the sea.

Fear seemed to have vanished and given way to a sense of challenge. The evening had noticeably cooled down and it was slipping inside our city skins. Still, I didn't dare invite her in. Lost in vague musings I noticed she was shaking. Without another thought I asked her in, compelling her to walk in front of me. I wanted to take care of every detail, every stitch of the filigree.

"I thought we were never coming in," she said. "Do you keep a secret in here or what?" I smiled, ashamed.

I lit the fire and we sat facing the fireplace, as if no time had elapsed since the first time we were here. But now we were alone.

The fire started roaring; Genovesa lit a cigarette. I couldn't think of anything but her mouth, her voice. She said it seemed incredible that we were alone together with nothing but walls around us.

Our glances became more and more intimate. Tensions began to disappear and we talked about ourselves, sitting comfortably on the cushions strewn on the floor.

I noticed she liked the stories I told her of my life. She demanded endings and beginnings; if something was missing she would stress it. Her way of talking was very different from mine: I spoke things out, she concealed mysteries under many veils. She took time in details, I saw the whole better. Our differences fascinated us.

"You know? I think love is essential for human beings," I said all of a sudden. "It's the best that can happen: everything finds meaning, everything becomes important and astonishing."

She smiled and said I was like a feminine version of Werther. To me she was la Maga of Cortazar. We laughed. I wanted to read her the thousand-times-read Chapter Seven in *Rayuela*. She accepted, delighted.

My eyes betrayed my feelings; it was difficult for her to endure the way I looked at her. Her gaze turned misty.

The heat had returned to our bodies and soon we began taking our clothes off. These seeming flirtations, caused by the temperature change, pushed desire to its limits, making me almost lose my judicious conduct.

Just then the telephone rang—as if to remind us that life existed *extramuros*, outside our walls. It was Alejandro landing like a black bird inside our closed circle. He wanted to know what had happened to me. "You're not the same," he complained.

He didn't understand what was going on and felt I owed him an explanation. I said I simply didn't want to see him; we would talk about it after the holiday was over.

"We'll talk about it right now!" he interrupted. "I have the right to know. I'm a man: nobody makes a fool of me."

I tried to be kind but my words were coming out violently.

Meanwhile, Genovesa had walked away and was wandering around the house. I saw how she was again attracted to the mirror arrangement with the carrousel as its central theme.

"No, of course you have no rights over me. I'm not your wife and even if I were..." I yelled and hung up abruptly.

Genovesa turned to look at me.

"Is that the guy you were going to marry?" she asked, her voice full of irony.

"No, I really wasn't going to marry him...or anybody. With my male lovers I never last longer than six months," I confessed.

"And with women?"

"With women? I'll tell you after I close the doors and windows."

"Why? do you think we're not safe in here? ¡*Cadena y candado!* Lock and chain!" she repeated in a hoarse voice, as I started down the lovers' staircase.

Outside everything was dark. I was scared the way I used to be when I was a child. I kept lighting every lamp on the way.

I stepped outside into the garden and cut the only red velvety rose that was left.

When I came back to the room, I found Genovesa sitting placidly amid the scattered cushions on the floor. She was looking for something in her handbag.

"Would you like a mint?" she asked.

47

THE MINT

Genovesa offered me a mint. I took it shamelessly with my mouth. I felt the unknown touch of her fingers on my tongue; a line of light opened a path through my brain. She jerked but didn't pull her hand away. I moved towards her mouth that was half open in surprise. I trembled, we both trembled. With my heart beating madly, I slipped my tongue into her mouth, I circled around her teeth. She tasted like a newly opened flower. Our glances parted like two birds in flight. We lost ourselves in the mirror that faced the bed. There were thousands of eyes filled with blue. In the center: two women, one kneeling before the other. Around them a cemetery of eyes, the sea, worms and waste.

The intensity of our feelings frightened us. We sank into a harsh silence. I saw my deep insides: black bowels turning red; small, red veins crossing my eyes. Genovesa was still fastened to the mirror. Wild flowers filled her eyes.

Everything lasted an instant but it seemed like eternity to me.

Her gaze slowly returned from the screen of reflections with a sadness that was a thousand years old. I could see myself in her as the young woman I had been not long ago. I held her hand: we each came from such different worlds...but somehow we were alike.

"It's not easy to shun our ancestral ghosts," I said. "What we are doing means that the oldest symbols, the ones we were given even before birth, have to be replaced...and we must find new ones."

"Yes," she said softly. She bowed her head and pulled the quilt over her legs. "I feel it has to do with something very old."

A sadness came over me. When she noticed I was distant, she brushed her hand over my cheek and asked if all this worried me too.

48

"Yes," I said. And my assertion seemed to calm her down.

Slowly our hard edges began to dissolve and clear desire returned.

She gave herself slowly. You had to caress her with your eyes; take away the sadness that concealed her voluptuousness. You had to do it delicately, like the fine traces of a Chinese watercolor. I licked her neck, her mouth....

Outside a fine rain was falling. The music of Alain Barriére welcomed us into our new territory. Two women, I thought with desire in every pore. My mouth lingered on her neck, I went down to her belly, holding her hips. She passed her breasts over mine, over my face, my mouth; her tongue stroked my neck. We found each others' mouths again, recognizing our tongues. I felt the pulse beating from my temples to my sex. The horses, oh god, gallop at the speed of wind, red flames bursting from their muzzles. Our bodies dance.

"How strong," she whispered.

"I want to make you mine...be yours," I murmured in her ear.

My excited tongue wanders over her breasts, her inflamed nipples, her smooth belly. It slides into her vulva: she is fresh moss inside. Silvery sparks fall over an iron sea. I feel so strong, boundless.

"I fear the vertigo," she said.

We hold each other; the earth turns liquid. She recognizes her own taste in my mouth.

While the logs crackle dryly in the fireplace our voices speak of love. A cosmopolitan voice says "I love you." That voice is mine and no one else's.

TO LIFE!

When I woke, I saw her lying by my side. She was very beautiful. I liked that she was only twenty-five and that she was there, sleeping peacefully in my bed. Her mouth stirred as if she were going to say something, but it was only dream's whispers. I wished this *Puente de Muertos* would never end. I've been waiting for her all my life, I thought. But she was a woman, and that was not easy to reconcile.

I remembered the times Morena had refused to introduce me to her cousin. In the end, before leaving, she finally had. She had also left Genovesa a note asking her to call me. They were so different. With Morena I had always been protective; but Genovesa, fourteen years younger than me, could show me new ways. With her I felt secure.

She opened her eyes and by her look I could tell something was wrong.

"We've been together two days," she said. "What's going to happen when the holiday is over?"

"Why worry now?" I said. "I like you."

She brushed her hand across the nape of my neck and shoulder.

"You have beautiful hands," I said.

She looked at them closely as if they were not hers. "They look like the hands of a painter," I added.

"And what do painters' hands look like?"

"I don't know, but yours are very sensitive."

She asked to see mine. She said she wouldn't know whose they were like, but definitely not a sociologist's. "What would you like to be?"

"A writer."

"Oh really? I wouldn't have guessed, you've kept it so quiet."

50

"I swear, I've wanted to be a writer all my life. I've studied acting, stage direction, sociology—all of it, to be able to write someday. But it seems as if time has drifted by too fast. I don't think I could start at my age."

"Why not? But you must leave everything and get started right away," she urged.

"I'll write a love story."

"Yes? Is there one that's very important in your life?" she asked without letting her tone betray her feelings. I kissed her and said ours was the most important story in my life. She asked how could I tell when I hardly knew her.

"I can tell. That's the advantage of age: love strikes like lightning and you know this is the person you've been longing for."

"I haven't lived long enough to know," she mused. She said she wasn't sure what she wanted from life. It worried her that her great love story might be with a woman. "It's not the most common thing in the world," she smiled. Besides, I was the mother of two sons and the daughter of well-known parents.

"So I'm not supposed to live the life I've always longed for? I'll surely end up old and bitter. My sons will soon get married and me, should I marry someone I don't love? How unfair."

"It would seem unfair to me too."

She brushed her hand over my breasts; for the first time she dared touch me before I touched her. Her mouth opened slightly and I could feel her wet tongue. I thrust mine out, asking for hers; this excited her madly and she pulled me on top of her, holding my waist. We kissed until we lost our breath.

51

THE SINISTER
SHOWS HIS HAND

The mirrors reflected our naked bodies. A ray of sun, like a cat's tongue, slipped through a slit in the shutters.

That morning Genovesa looked like a young animal that has shed its tensions playing love games. She opened one eye, then the other; noticed that I was watching her and woke with a start. I kissed her softly to remind her who I was. She clung to me like a pampered cat and we gave each other the first kiss of the morning. We rolled in bed hugging and ended up on the African rug, watching the embers of last night's fire. We made love just to feel one another again.

Now that we had trespassed beyond the limits, I suggested we go out on the terrace. She accepted, saying she always loved seeing my beautiful plants. I pulled a couple of strident-yellow mattresses out of the terrace shed and sprawled them on the brick floor. She was off admiring the flowers again.

"Come see! They're blooming more this morning," she shouted. "They're happier."

We played with the words: blooming, happier; *más abiertas, más felices. Las pusimos, las antepusimos, las pospusimos, las propusimos.* We put words down, placed them before and after; turned them around. "There are so many possibilities," she uttered, placidly stretched out on the mattress. She closed her eyes; the sun shone directly on her face. Then she wanted to touch me. She pulled herself up and sat. She moved her finger across my lips, drew their contours. I touched her finger with the tip of my tongue.

Ay! my mouth became a cave, her finger wanted to discover all its crevices: to come in and look, and come out, and come in again....I pulled her down, slid my tongue along her back, caressed her well formed waist, her butt.

"Your hands are like small birds," she said. A gust of wind made the weeping willows sway.

She turned, anxiously looking for my mouth. We kissed. She stroked the curve of my back. I felt her nipples hardening under the soft pressure of my lips. Her hips swayed up and down, I threw her legs apart with my knee and our rhythms coupled. She passed her hand over my breasts, went back to my waist. She turned me over so she could ride on my back. Her mane covered my face; through this golden screen I looked up and saw cotton clouds traveling fast across the sky. We rolled, we swayed and spun. I put my fingers on her clitoris; with my thigh I helped my hand. She was stroking my arm and whispering "more, more, more"; her whispers turned into a moan, into a scream, into peels of laughter. An inexpressible pleasure burst open.

The sun hid under a cloud. She sought out my vagina anxiously. The sun came out again so we wouldn't be cold. An iridescent light pierced me...she was moving rhythmically in and out. The world of all beginnings, I was thinking, as I heard a strange noise. I saw a thousand sea shells breaking. "Wait, stop," I commanded.

I rushed to the terrace to look down on the street and saw Alejandro climbing the gate. In a second I was inside again and telling Genovesa. She didn't understand what was going on. I took her hand and, naked as she was, led her to the shed and shut the door on her. I went back into the bedroom and slipped on the bathrobe that was lying on the bed.

Alejandro was already outside the bedroom door knocking furiously. Luckily the bolt was drawn. Ay, my pounding heart....

I opened the door with my mind set on....He stepped in glancing at me dismissively as if he owned the house. How dare he! I thought. He walked straight through to the dressing room, opened the bathroom door and looked in. He came back, turned the key to the antique wardrobe door and then noticed the seven flower vases filled with roses. He turned to look at me. I wished I had the guts to throw him out.

In the midst of this hatred, he tripped and inadvertently pushed the upstairs switch that turned the carrousel on. A band of horns blared out noisily. He shrieked like a rat caught in a trap.

"What's this? A madhouse?"

When I saw him stepping out onto the terrace I choked with terror.

"So this is it," he said, pointing to the yellow mattresses. *"Aquí hay gato encerrado,* something's fishy here," he added.

His dark glasses gleamed in the light. He headed straight for the storeroom, held the doorknob between his fingers. I wanted to cry, "Wait! There're spiders in there." Uf! he changed his mind at the last moment and dropped his hand from the knob.

"You're getting out of here, right now!" I hissed and rushed inside. I picked up a pair of ancient stones from my collection and, holding them over my head, threatened to break his skull if he didn't go. He backed away cursing. I walked him downstairs to open the gate. I made him return the keys I had given him and slammed the door so hard that he must have been flung into the middle of the street.

I rushed upstairs to get Genovesa out of the storeroom. She was buckled over and pale.

"Did he leave already?" she asked dryly.

I could tell immediately that something in her was broken. She couldn't understand the kind of woman I was. How was it possible that the man had keys to the house and I hadn't taken any precautions? I tried to explain that he had jumped over the gate and that lock and key were usually enough.

She wasn't interested in explanations and asked abruptly when the rest of the family were coming back.

"Tonight, probably."

"So it's time for me to go."

The world seemed to turn over. She asked me to come with her into the dressing room. I sat on the rug and watched her pack her brown night bag. She looked like an angry child.

"You can't go like this," I exclaimed. "There must be something I can say to persuade you to stay. It wouldn't be fair for the story."

"What story?"

I told her I was certain that she was using this as an excuse to flee and not confront what had happened between us. She set her bag down and came to sit by my side. She turned to look at me and I realized I was on the right track.

"You really think so?"

I slipped my hand under her white shirt. She pulled it out and held it in midair.

"You're dangerous," she stated.

A SMALL BRIGHT MOON

Calm settled in again after the incident. We were captivated by the themes of the mind: fear of loving, fear of living, guilt. But desire went beyond every fear.

I took a drag of the joint her dear cousin had left me to enjoy when the right time came...and the right time had come. Tomorrow was my birthday, I would be older: many years old. And that granted me permission to enjoy it all.

My astrologer, a Basque man who had settled in Tepoztlán, had just revealed to me that my skies were very propitious and that the heavenly bodies had shaped a splendorous star of David on the day I was born. He also discovered that a comet had shone past it.

"This dazzling phenomenon occurred on a cold winter morning," I said.

Stunned by my astral beginnings, Genovesa let herself be conducted to bed and we spent the day and night among warm and well-rewarded feelings.

"It won't be easy to say goodbye in the middle of such radiant cosmology," she confessed in a moment of clarity when she woke. "Happy birthday, love, happy birthday." She gave me a blue teapot and a book of poems by Cavafy.

"It's time we face the fierce outside," I suggested.

We hadn't gone out of the house in three days, so we had to shed the feline sensations that too many love games had left.

My black Mustafá was ready for a downtown expedition and we backed away from the house with a flourish.

It was the first time we were leaving our territory.

As we drove down Reforma Avenue, I told her I used to go out on Sundays with my father when I was a child. I pointed to the dahlias that flowered on the *camellones*. "On these lawns horsemen, dressed as *charros,* used to ride beautiful horses."

56

"On Reforma? I don't believe it."

"As we watched them passing by, my father always said he'd buy a horse. He didn't mind his scar then, but my mother would scold him. She'd argue that my brother or I would surely end up wanting one of those beasts. We would all keep quiet but I would secretly long to be the owner of a white mare someday."

Genovesa took my hand but let it drop immediately. We were out on the streets now for the first time, and we sensed the *gran familia*, the extended Mexican family traveling with us. Some were sitting on the trunk, others were hanging from the doors. They all pointed at us with their tiny fingers. "You've gone too far," they seemed to say.

Genovesa was looking ahead with a furrowed brow. I wanted to touch the golden down on her arms. She sensed my desire and I watched her breathing alter under her black and gold blouse. I kissed her mouth.

"It's downright impossible not to feel lust when you're near," she said.

"It's downright impossible not to feel. Period."

The balance left by the *Puente de Muertos* was two women in love.

"And what are we supposed to do now?" she asked. I answered back with another kiss. She kissed me hotly as the red light changed.

The driver in the car behind us started honking. We laughed and kissed until we reached Tacuba Street. By then our families and their values had vanished and we were immersed once more in what we felt for each other.

"There's room over there," she cried, pointing at a parking space. I managed to get Mustafá into the tight place in two movements. "You're good!" she clapped. *"Un as del volante!"*

At the Majestic Hotel, the elevator assistant observed us with curiosity. She asked if we were sisters.

"Just *sui generis* friends," Genovesa replied.

"Sui what?"

We stepped out on the penthouse's open terrace. The flag was being hoisted down on the Zócalo. We hadn't seen the ceremony before so we stood and watched. Far in the distance, the orange metro train sped by as if traveling along the edge of a building. I thought it must be a hallucination but Genovesa said she'd seen it too. I noticed that our eyes revealed the days we had just spent together.

We ordered tequila Conmemorativo and Black and White. I slipped my hand under the table and caressed her thigh. She got nervous, dropped the ashes of her cigarette and turned her eyes to the ceiling, blowing out smoke.

"It's a pity I can't kiss you," I said.

"But you are kissing me, I feel your mouth all over me," she mumbled, looking around to see if anybody was watching.

The drinks arrived. "Shall we toast for *los vivos* again?" I asked.

"Just for them," she said, and asked, "Have you been in love many times?" as if she had never asked the question before.

"It's the first time," I assured her.

She watched to see if I were lying, then turned to the window.

The sky suddenly darkened and, within seconds, a downpour began.

"Isn't it strange?" she said, puzzled. "It's not the rainy season anymore."

The window panes turned misty and the Cathedral domes vanished. All was submerged under the oranges and dark lilacs of dusk.

There was such a *pelotera*, a confusion in the streets, that I realized it would be difficult to leave. I said that I regretted we weren't in bed. "Me too," she said and slipped her leg between mine under the table.

The bartender switched on the radio. The weather newscast reported that the airport had been closed down. "This is incredible!" I cried out. "No one will be able to return from the holiday."

We would be having an island day just for ourselves.

We took all the detours back to our shelter. The storm had left a clear sky and a small bright moon.

At home, the mirrors gathered the light of the shimmering stars. We climbed upstairs. I turned on the carrousel and the wooden horses began their ritual. Sensuous Mina was singing on the record player. Genovesa glanced at herself in the entrance oval mirror. She slid her fingers through her hair; a reflection of coppers scattered through the bedroom and a voluptuous woman appeared.

"Come," I said. She approached as if she were obeying an order.

"Undress."

She started to take off her clothes, piece by piece, with her eyes fixed on mine. A circle of colors spread at her feet. I put the Philippine quilt around her naked shoulders and she began to unbutton my shirt. When she had finished, she turned her back on me and walked downstairs with tense calm. The clatter of my boots marked her steps. As she passed by, the mirrors multiplied her image. My heartbeat, which was usually slow, quickened. I followed.

She reached the carrousel and, without hesitating, climbed on Mahoma. Her hands gripped the axis. I mounted and wrapped my arms around her breasts. The quilt fell to the floor. Her shoulders shone with the light of a moon that was like a button-hole on a baby's blouse.

Mounted atop the black animal, in a fluid acrobatic movement she spun her pelvis as I watched, stunned by her skills. Now she was facing me and she clasped my neck. The music rose in crescendo. She lay back against Mahoma's neck. I kissed her firm breasts and went down to her belly. My tongue traveled the full journey to her vagina: it was a fig flower. Shreds of wind echoed through the music. The mirror—our accomplice—watched as I was reborn under the shadows of her pubis.

We woke in front of the fireplace with the red carnations of the quilt covering our bodies. A tinkling of metal made me rush out on the terrace. Agustín was pulling the chain out of its lock. My sons will soon be back too, I thought. Valeria, who had dreamed herself free, had to come down to earth.

Genovesa lay quietly in bed. I asked her to stay the night with me again.

"We'll decide later in the day," she said and furled herself around me. I went back to sleep, but I was restless and had a nightmare.

On the street outside the house of my dreams, I saw a man with a rope pulling a white horse by its neck. The animal tried to bite me; it was fierce. All of a sudden it escaped its owner's grip and started to chase me. I rushed to a neighbor's house and climbed the gate. The owner came out and I screamed it was me, the girl she knew well. "Please, let me in," I begged, but the woman wouldn't open the door. All the time the horse neighed, showing its bare teeth. I yelled.

Genovesa switched on the lights and held me tenderly.

"What's wrong? Don't cry, love, you make me sad."

She kissed me, nestling my head on her warm chest.

MY HORSES

Before he left for school, Alberto told me of his decision to go into my father's business. Soon he's going to be in charge of his fortune, I thought; I had ambivalent feelings about it. I didn't know if I should be glad or regretful, so I told him I was happy but worried as well.

"Businessmen are very ambitious, they need power to achieve what they want. They become callous and later they have to re-learn how to live. Your grandfather is the best example."

Alberto smiled as if what I was saying rang a bell, but what I thought wasn't so good he considered wonderful.

Genovesa arrived in the evening, full of passion and carrying flowers; all the bad omens vanished.

Later, we talked about my discussion with Alberto. The fact that one of my children would continue what my father had created seemed wonderful to her.

"I would have preferred something more sublime for my sons," I confessed.

"But they don't seem to want anything more sublime for themselves," she replied. "So there's nothing you can do."

She was right. I arranged the flowers in the vase.

After making love I invited her to meet my horses. "I love the idea," she said. So I called the stable and ordered them bathed and combed for the royal visit.

They were my father's gifts to me: Madona and Persona, two vigorous mares. "One for each grandson I gave him," I told her.

At the stable lockers, I pulled my tight, shiny black boots over my old jeans and picked up the light straw hat from its hook. I trotted Madona around the ring to show off my skills. Genovesa was watching intently.

"I'll lend you Persona, she's friendlier." But she elegantly refused.

"I've never been on a horse," she said, clasping her hands. "But they're so beautiful."

I smiled and maneuvered even more gracefully to convince her to ride with me. It took a while, but when she finally accepted, she jumped up and squeezed tight against me.

"Slowly, please, slowly," she kept saying. I felt her heart pounding against my back, a strong and steady beat.

The stables were located in the newest section of Chapultepec. Trotting lightly, we went all the way to the borders of Panteón Dolores, the cemetery. We climbed the hill among fresh flowers. Genovesa was suspicious of my intentions and thought the whole thing was sacrilegious.

We reached the top of a ravine where a river flowed during the rainy season. There were birds chirping and the wind coiled around the trees. I dismounted and helped Genovesa down. Madona whinnied as I tied her to a tree; Genovesa pulled me towards her. We kissed, falling on the high grass, and rolled down the slope until we hit bottom. As we descended, her shirt sleeve had caught on a branch and I licked the blood that dripped from her arm. In a rush of desire I tore her blouse and anxious, high in flight, tried to pull the zipper of her pants down.

"Not here," she said, stopping my hand.

I brushed my lips over her breasts, then went back to her mouth. I insisted with the zipper.

The color of the sky waned and the sour smell of old *zempasúchiles* rose with each new gust of wind.

Genovesa stopped resisting; I slipped my hand inside her underpants and touched her wetness: it was a sea. We were madly kissing when I suddenly heard the noise of an engine a few feet above us. A car was going by slowly without its headlights on.

"It's a police car," I whispered. She was about to rush off, meteor-like, but I grabbed her foot and stopped her. "Hush, don't move," I ordered. Madona, dark as the night, remained unseen and the patrol car moved on without a clue we were there. We both sighed with relief.

"Let's get out of here!" she urged. My constant drive for adventure got on her nerves.

We took the black mare back to her quarters. "We're not free," I assured her, kissing the star on Madona's forehead. "We must endure our fate."

62

Genovesa stroked the spot where I had stamped my kiss.

"Don't heed her," she said to the horse, "all things are bound to change."

Mustafá was waiting outside the horse stables. "Straight to bed!" I commanded.

CONCEALING THE
ORIGINAL PURPOSE

A whole month had gone by and we weren't able to be apart. Desire was stronger, *nos ganaba la pasión,* and our plans to leave one another never lasted long. I smiled: the kidnapping had turned into reality.

I parked Mustafá in front of her building. It was earlier than we had agreed. From the strategic place where I stood, I could watch her painting. She put a brush mark on the canvas, drew away from it, then paced back and forth, repeating this operation again and again. I realized she was veiling her original intentions with firm strokes of the brush.

In a minute when I wasn't paying attention, the lights of the studio were switched off. The brown-skinned woman vanished to get dressed and made-up. She had a date with her lover. A month already, she was telling herself.

She disappeared into the inner rooms where I couldn't see her. She glanced sideways at her face in the bathroom mirror, stuck her tongue out and watched its surface encircled by teeth. She took out her makeup kit, red with yellow dots, and spread out a number of theatre makeup jars on top of the washbasin. The transvestite prince appeared on her mental screen.

Two girls were walking amidst discarded skins and false gold dentures. The urban landscape swarmed with multicolored fish that glided inside dry aquariums. Genovesa wandered among her ghosts.

She opened the can of crushed gold and applied it in great quantities to her upper lids. She drew a line around the edge of her lower lids and daubed her eyelashes with matte black.

Then she highlighted her cheekbones to isolate them from the rest of her face and retouched the eyeshadow which gave her eyes a glow of sensuous magic.

She returned to the studio and switched on the lights, aware of her sensual looks and feeling extra-young.

I rang the doorbell then and climbed swiftly upstairs. She was leaning on the door frame waiting with a red shawl over her naked torso.

We rushed inside the unfurnished apartment, anxious for each other. The doors to all the rooms were closed and I imagined they were secret passageways. The red rose bouquet I had sent was resting in a corner.

We sat on our appointed stools; the mirror cast back our reflections. Insubstantial clouds changed form outside the window. A full moon hovered, in my mind, over a blue sea of nostalgia. She glanced at me and covered her eyes as if struck by lightning.

"Our eyes look exactly the same," she uttered, alarmed.

"Your desire reflects in my eyes, that's why."

"I think your desire is contagious...yes, I'm positive."

She climbed down from the stool and came to caress my face, closing her eyes so I could admire the mastery of her makeup.

"I love you, Valeria."

She had never pronounced my name, and now that she did, I had a chain reaction of inexpressible feelings, amber lights, stars in my mind.

"I love you," I murmured faintly as we kissed passionately.

She held my shoulders and glanced inadvertently in the mirror.

For a minute I had the impression she wanted to smash the surface. She was looking at her painting. It's the ocean of her dreams that upsets her, I thought.

I told her she had the quality of a shooting star. "You're hard to grasp," I admitted.

"With you, life is a risk," she said. "One must learn to take flight."

Flight and desire linked in a luminous act. She squeezed her body against mine, kissed my neck and slipped her tongue into my ear, exploring as if it were full of mysterious nooks. I caressed her breasts, yielding.

The church bells struck eleven; shooting star and taker unfolded.

"Let's go to my bedroom," she said.

We made love in the same narrow bed in which we hadn't slept a wink the first night we lay together.

"Times change," she observed, as we heard the hieratic sound of the bells striking three.

"Hurry, dress! I want us to go hear *boleros* at the Noche y Día."

"First we take a hot shower," she said coquettishly.

"We take…and give whatever you like."

Eva, the eternal waitress, received us at the door as old *habitues*. The guitar player came over to our table and sang old romantic *boleros*. Genovesa was delighted. "I love you," she kept repeating. I told her I was absolutely happy at her side. "To love," we toasted.

Virgin Mary! It was six o'clock in the morning by Eva's watch. We hurried out of the restaurant holding hands.

Ricky was coming out of the house, ready to leave for school. He stared at us. Genovesa wanted to get out of the car but I held her back.

"What are you doing out so early?" he asked, glancing again at Genovesa. "Or is it so late?"

"We're going for our morning walk, all the way to the Desierto de los Leones," I replied, trying to look calm.

"At six in the morning?" my son wanted to know.

He started his Firebird and drove off with the gas pedal to the floor, imitating my style of driving.

RESTRICTED FREEDOM

I imagined her entering her studio with the nightbag in her hand. She looked at her empty place and compared it to my house of baroque tastes.

Every morning now she packed her things in that damned brown bag and left for her studio. When she was gone, I was left with the feeling that she didn't know if she would be coming back to me.

The fact that I was the mother of two teenage sons and the daughter of a prominent family was sometimes too much for her. She had told me so more than once. "How much longer can our relationship last?" she would ask. I would tell her, as long as we wanted it to.

"No one can prevent us from loving each other and wanting to be together," I would say. "Our own internalized fears are worse than real prohibitions."

She would disagree, saying we couldn't keep the relationship going much longer. "It's going to be harder as time goes on."

Her pessimism that morning made us fight. "It's precisely what you lack that I have more of than I need, my dear," I cried, enraged at her lack of spirits. "If you want to go, go. I won't die, even if I cry oceans of tears. You know that."

My attitude annoyed her. She told me I was acting like an adolescent who didn't want to face reality.

"If I dared look at what I have to face in order to love you, I would surely flee in terror," I asserted.

She didn't answer, but she left with her brown bag anyway.

I remained desolate, sure that she wouldn't return. But she must have known. She called me to keep me from hurting.

As we were talking, an unexpected rush of desire took us unaware: we were two passionate women, after all.

"Come see me," she said, laughing.

After we made love she asked, "Why can't I stop being afraid and just live my love for you fully?"

It was getting late. We dressed hurriedly to be in time for her class. She gave art lessons to children. She liked her work, and what was more important, it gave her financial independence.

"As a painter you can starve," she would say, laughing bitterly. "And this job, who knows? Maybe it won't last long, now that the crisis in México is getting worse."

The children came running to say hello. "Today we'll paint the jungle animals," she explained when the excitement waned a little. She pulled out little buckets from the cabinets, filled them with water and gave the children cans of paint of all different colors.

A few minutes later, a little girl with short curly hair came over and pulled her hand. She wanted to show Genovesa the giraffe she had just painted. Genovesa stooped to look at the drawing and hugged the girl. "It's beautiful," she said, pointing to the yellow giraffe. She kissed her tenderly.

Suddenly the thought hit me that being with me meant she was missing her opportunity to be a mother. And she had the tenderness and the strength to be a wonderful mother.

I felt something choking my throat and tears rushed to my eyes. I went to her and said that I would wait outside; she asked if I was feeling all right.

"Yes, I just need some fresh air. I'm tired."

"Don't go far," she urged, sensing something. "I won't be long."

When the class was over, we drove to The Opera, the old bar downtown. Although entrance to *cantinas* was not forbidden to women anymore, we were the only ones there. We had noticed that the food in these places was as good as in first-class restaurants and half the price.

The waiter brought us to *un apartado:* an enclosed table where we could sit by ourselves undisturbed. Genovesa smiled at him.

After the drinks had been served, I told her what had crossed my mind during the class; how it had saddened me.

"Yes, I've thought about that too," she said. "But I figure it's one of those things I'll have to deal with when the time comes." Meanwhile, she had a few more years ahead of her; she needn't worry yet. "Let's not get sad," she comforted. And the *apartado* served its purpose.

SURPRISE PARTY

The woman with the fiery breast fanned her long hair. She shaped a prison with her fingers, looked through the mesh. She discovered a sophisticated woman getting ready to leave the house. She leaned on the cold stone column and thought about the differences between herself and the other.

"Ay, *oaxacavidamía*, I must hurry."

Genovesa threw her head back and the veins of her neck showed. I went and bit them softly, leaving a subtle mark on her skin. She put her hand on my shoulder and said, "You're very late, you know. How will you get there at midnight?"

"That's exactly what I'm asking myself, and worse, how can I show up at my parents' with this happy face?"

I put on the last touches of makeup in front of the mirror and looked at my profile. My elegance was flawless.

"Tell me, will you be the same when you come back?" she asked, looking steadily into my eyes.

"When I come back I'll be your Valeria."

"Sharing with the family might..." the phrase remained suspended in the air.

I walked past her with the scent of *Odalisque Troisieme* and a De la Renta dress bought especially for the event. We kissed a last time.

Dressed in this ambivalent disguise, I imagined I was going to a masquerade. I climbed into the car; it was a harsh winter evening. Leonard Cohen sang on the radio, "Mother, I'm frightened of the thunder and the lightning. I'll never be able to go through."

"I'm scared too," I told him as I slammed on the brakes in front of my parents' house in a skillful tailspin.

The mansion, built in the style of *Gone With the Wind,* was all lit up. My father's bodyguard took my car. In the hall, next to

70

a life-size statue playing the harp, I glanced in the mirror. I'm still attractive, I thought.

The music of "Le Nouveau Monde" filled the room. I held the muscles of my stomach tight, concentrated on the lowest notes of the orchestra, and entered the main parlor with a distracted demeanor.

Just as I crossed the threshold I met my mother's eye. "Late as always," she mouthed through glossy lips *a la* Ceylon Night. There was a time when one of her looks was all I needed to understand what she wanted from me, and I would act accordingly. But this was no longer true. I waved my hand from a distance.

Fine ladies and elegant gentlemen swallowed caviar tidbits and Brazilian hearts of palm. Andrés, the house waiter, brought me a glass of ice-cold Polish vodka. Luis Sandoval escaped his wife to come and say hello. He wanted to tell me all about his trip to the South Seas. "Have you ever been there?" he asked.

"No."

"It's the most beautiful place on earth. We should go there together," he whispered with a lustful look in his eyes.

He asked why I didn't go to the flamenco class he had invited me to.

"Engagements, trips, and frankly I don't see myself *zapateando*, stamping my feet."

"You're wrong; you'd look divine."

He seized the moment—adopted a gypsy look, lifted his hands above his head and conjured up blood and carnations. Shouting "olé!" he tapped, *"tacón y punta, tacón y punta."*

Oh, god! Everyone had turned around to look. "Olé," I echoed as I took little sips of my vodka.

"You're so beautiful!" he murmured hurriedly when he saw his "pussy cat" approaching.

I slipped away to kiss lawyer Limantour's wife. She had the appearance of a distinguished lady from Don Porfirio's times.

"If the mountain doesn't come to Mohammed..." my mother said, turning her cheek to be kissed.

My father had stayed behind chatting with a friend, a former banker like himself, whom he respected for his shrewdness.

71

"You want to know something?" my father said, with a look of nostalgia. "When I was poor and dreamed of being a millionaire, I used to sleep like a bull. Now that I'm rich, I don't sleep."

Life's paradoxes, I thought. Ay, I had always believed he would never get old.

Just then an attractive woman drew near. "*Aquí, sólo mis chicharrones truenan*. At my feet, I'm the queen," she seemed to say with a self-satisfied smile. She was Refugio Alvarez. My mother had always thought she was a tramp but admired her wit.

The conversation spun around the theft of her jewels from the Hotel Ritz in Paris. She spoke at length about it.

"That evening," she said faintly, "Jorge and I were very tired, so we went down for dinner at the hotel restaurant. By the way, if you haven't been there, go, next time you visit Paris, it's divine...," she glanced at me. "Well, when we went back to our room the robbers were already there waiting for us, can you imagine? They tied Jorge's hands and feet, stuck a handkerchief inside his mouth and then knocked him unconscious," she added remorsefully.

"Poor man," Mrs. Limantour whispered, imagining the scene.

"I wasn't tied, beaten or anything," Refugio smiled slyly. "They made a careful selection of my jewels and took away the best," she added, sighing deeply. "No," she said annoyed, "there's no doubt these French crooks are first class."

My mother sympathized but I noticed a look in her eyes that said something didn't quite fit.

"But we're not too concerned," Refugio said. "The Interpol is already on their track." Then she turned to me. "And you, where have you been hiding?"

"Oh, I only..." It was better to avoid the subject, asking her out for lunch to some celestial place like Las Mañanitas in Cuernavaca instead. "So we can have a long, intimate chat," I lied.

"Uy, I would like that," she said, gesturing like Maria Félix under *palmeras borrachas de sol*. Her black eyes sparkled.

All of a sudden the lights on the ceiling, with its finely carved wooden lattice from India, were turned down. The sounds of a fanfare echoed through the house. My brother and his new wife—a Swedish-looking blonde, who was a head taller than him—entered the room. The first-born was turning forty-six; he had just had a face lift and looked like an old child. My father looked at the floor, regretting that his only son was not fit to take over his empire. My mother nudged him; my father applauded. I made an effort not to laugh.

The honored one was sweating profusely amidst so many greetings and embraces. When a tray passed at eye level, I picked up a glass of white wine. The greetings ended at the same time I deposited my empty glass on another tray. Now it's my turn, I told myself. I placed a heavy Chagall art book in his hands.

"I've got it already," he said, "but thanks, anyway."

Merde allors, he wouldn't take his eyes off some fixed spot behind my head. I turned to see what had caught his attention. Before I realized what it was, he had walked around me to straighten a Tamayo painting on the wall. Asshole, I thought.

The violins started playing a sad blues, Greenwich Village-style. Andrés came over to pour some fresh vodka in my glass. What am I doing here without her? I asked myself, and without hesitation I went to call her on the phone.

"I know an impetuous lady who sends electric charges from my spine down to my vagina."

Genovesa breathed hard.

"You're not sleeping, are you? Wait for me, I won't be long. I want you near me, your female thighs around my waist, I want to make you laugh, uy, I want..."

She flared up, excited, and yelled, "Shut up or I'm going to come!"

Click.

Someone had been listening on the other end of the line!

"Wait for me, I'm going to look for the corpse," I said and hung up the receiver.

Who was the son of a bitch who had listened to our conversation? Perhaps my brother; perhaps my mother. I was suddenly dry as a desert; happiness vanished from my face. I decided to leave right away, as if nothing had happened. As I was going out, I recalled my mother's words: "Your father would die if you did something wrong." I left without saying goodbye to anyone, in the midst of a dark vertigo.

When I returned home, Genovesa was waiting up for me. She said she wanted me and helped me get undressed. Her kisses slid down my body like fine velvet. She squeezed my waist between her thighs and glued herself to my belly. With her legs astride she humped my back.

"Up and down, up and down," she repeated, pausing to kiss me each time.

"*Siete, aldaba, pez.* Seven, latch, fish," I screamed, as if these were the words of an incantation. Her gaze was lost in an abyss.

"Are you still the guardian of shooting stars?" she asked.

"I'm still the same," I whispered in her ear.

She turned to kiss me again, leisurely; she ascended until her vulva reached my lips. My tongue moved along her clitoris and into the deepness; an indigo planetary light shimmered. My throat emitted a newly found sound: ay, ay, ay! I flew across the immensity of the cosmos. I had never, ever felt what I felt with her.

A sip of wine; cheese and bread and more salad; on the bed, on the rug, in front of the fireplace, out on the terrace, under the moon, with the trees humming in the wind, next to the locusts' chant.

When passion finally diminished, we fell asleep immediately. Later in the night I had a frightful dream. I watched two tin soldiers marching in. One was dressed in blue and gold, the other had a red and silver uniform. They drew their swords, preparing for battle. The one in blue, whom I recognized as myself for the way he proudly held his head, lunged into the other's stomach. The wounded soldier fell to the ground. The other one approached to make sure he had killed him. When he was certain he had, he turned away, letting the flies move in.

I couldn't sleep anymore after I woke. Genovesa hugged me and asked me what was happening.

"I know I belong to the tribe of Cain," I said, crying. "I always believed I would die by my brother's hand, but in the dream, it was the opposite. It was I who struck the mortal blow."

I was ashamed to have woken Genovesa again. I said I'd try not to do it anymore. "I'm revealing all my weak spots to you."

"Don't worry," she replied tenderly, "perhaps it's good that you get rid of your fears instead of always acting so strong."

DISCREPANCIES
IN THE BATH

The steam rising from the bathtub made the tropical leaves seem like sea tentacles. We were listening to the climax of Beethoven's *Leonora*. While we bathed in the warm waters of this inner pool, Genovesa pulled off the bath cap she was wearing. I gave her wine to drink, mouth to mouth. I asked her to wait for me a moment and stood up to get out of the tub.

"Out of place," she said, embracing me, trying to bring me back into the water.

I swore I wouldn't take long. I thought out each step. I brought back the instrument that freezes moments. I opened the tripod at the edge of the bathtub and ran to her side. The kiss lasted longer than the click.

"Did you know Fassbinder died yesterday?" she asked.

"How do you know?"

"I heard about it on Radio Educación."

We talked about this German genius, about his homosexuality. "How sad that he died so young, I'm going to miss him," she said.

The death of the movie director led us directly to talk about Nazi Germany. Looking at our reflections in the misty mirror, I joked that for us it would have been twice as bad: because we were Jewish and because we loved each other.

Genovesa didn't appreciate my acid sense of humor. She said we shouldn't play around with such things.

"Besides, you wouldn't have had a thing to worry about, because you look exactly like Petra Von Kant," she said.

"And you, you look exactly like her perverse lover."

We laughed, relieved. Without any transition we began discussing the economic crisis in México. Obviously, dark times surrounded us. Genovesa, who had recently joined the lines of the unemployed, wondered where it would all lead.

"To a paramilitary state, where else? But you shouldn't worry, we will live together in this house."

"With your children? Don't be crazy. They would lynch me."

This time I changed the subject, pulling her towards me. I dived below the hot waters and kissed her belly.

In the middle of this subaquatic scene the intercom buzzed. I ran out to the dressing room to answer. It was my son Ricky. He wanted to know the meaning of *discrepancy*.

"To disagree with something," I answered after thinking a moment.

"Well, I disagree," he said emphatically. "And besides, we're going out for dinner."

"Who's we?" I asked.

"Marcos and me."

Ricky walks out through the dining room. He stops in front of the glass cabinet to stare at the menorah that my mother had given me as a wedding present. He tries to pull it out but the small door won't open; he searches for the key but can't find it. He shatters the glass with an elbow and takes hold of it. I hear his footsteps on the staircase as he comes up to my bedroom. I go out to receive him, dripping wet. He raises the menorah above his head as high as he can and smashes it over my head.

Genovesa lifted me from the floor and pulled me to the bed like a heavy burden. She covered me with a towel. My forehead was bleeding like a fountain.

"Ay, auch, uuy," I moaned.

"Shut up," she said, kissing me softly. "Promise me one thing, that you will never, ever go with wet feet again to answer the intercom. Do you hear me?"

"Only if you give me another little kiss...but uyy...be very careful."

NEW YORK

Facing the window of the Stan-
hope, turned into a silhouette, I sat watching the last of the
delicate snowflakes fall on the gray pavement. The sky was now
an undisturbed blue and awakened my hopes that it wasn't so
unseasonably cold outside. But reddened faces shattered my
illusions as people rushed by the windows of the bar.

It had all started the night before, when Genovesa and I
arrived in New York. We had invited her friend Amy to have dinner
with us. Genovesa, a little drunk, confessed to her that loving a
woman was only a stage she had to go through. Amy had smiled
as if reassured.

"Valeria is the one who'll get hurt," Amy had said, fixing her
blue eyes on me.

I hadn't uttered a word, not even when we were alone.
Genovesa had wanted to know what was wrong with me, but I
was already anchored in one of my unbreakable silences. She fell
asleep as if nothing had happened. Why shouldn't she, if I was
only a stage in her life?

A zigzagging lightning bolt died in front of the window. The
waiter asked if I cared for another vodka. I nodded. He made a
comment to the bartender and I noticed they were both looking
at me.

When we woke up I had decided to put aside my rage and
keep up with our plans to visit the Whitney Museum. She had
talked to me on the plane about the artist Edward Hopper. She
wanted to show me her favorite painting by him, "Room Facing
the Ocean."

We walked out the door. "Good day, beautiful ladies," the
hotel porter bade us farewell.

"Good day," I answered with a British accent.

77

Even though it was early May the cold was intense. Genovesa wasn't certain she wanted to go to the museum after all.

"Do you ever know what you want?" I cried out, annoyed.

"Do I have to tell you each morning that I'm madly in love with you?"

I burst out saying I didn't want to go any place with her. Fifth Avenue spread open into parallel sidewalks; we each went separate ways. There was one direction for cars and various options for the pedestrian. Go where? I asked myself. Where without her? All clarity vanished.

I walked adrift. The winds blew down the funnel streets; the cold seeped into my lungs. The possibility that Genovesa could leave my life with impunity frightened me. Valeria is only a stage in my life—these damn words resounded in the suffocating aisles of my pyramidal body.

All of a sudden, I was certain she was following me. I turned around quickly to surprise her. But there was nobody there. Desolate, I kept on walking. I tried to remember exactly what had made us fight, but it was lost in the darkness of my memory.

The buildings joined at the sky. Suddenly there she was, on the opposite sidewalk, walking against the wind. The lapel of her jacket was pulled up against her neck. I saw an oblique glance, like a reptile's, appear on her profiled face.

I'm sure she's been following me the whole time, I thought. She'll cross the street and come to ask my forgiveness. I want to walk with you, she'll say. Naturally I will not accept; she is a woman incapable of loving.

When I turned again to look for her, she was not there. I began to cry. A frozen tear fell on the sidewalk. I stepped on it with my sneaker.

Hundreds of eyes were fixed on my face; eyes that meant nothing to me. I saw her once more. Genovesa was talking to a woman dressed in elegant furs. Is she asking if she has seen her lover? The woman pointed down the street and Genovesa thanked her with a little bow.

She walked fast. At the street corner she hesitated, not sure where to turn. My sharp eye was following her. Genovesa climbed the step and got lost in the revolving door of the Whitney. How could she? I thought. How could she go in without me?

I decided to find a bookstore and lose myself among the new releases. I saw everything with her eyes; nothing could hold my attention for more than a second. Suddenly my gaze was caught by Barthes' *Camera Lucida*. Right beside it I found *A Boy's Own Story* by Edmund White. I had just read a review of it the day before. In the book, a terrified adolescent boy confronts his supermacho father. I thought about the story's resemblance to my own life. Then suddenly a magical sign: I saw the bookseller making room for an art book on Hopper that had just come out...hot off the press. I went straight to it. My hands trembled as I looked for the picture Genovesa loved. I imagined us standing together beside the original: the room with its open door facing a petrified ocean.

I imagine how I can change the course of destiny if, right now, I walk into the museum and wait in front of the painting. When Genovesa walks by it, she will think I'm part of the scenery. She'll surely believe it's a hallucination. She'll come closer and, realizing it's me, she will embrace and kiss and hug me....I rushed out of the bookstore.

Outside everything had turned monochromatic. People were running as if they were in a hurry to get somewhere. I too hurried...into a bar.

The waiter brought me another vodka. I took several gulps of the transparent liquid but I couldn't find any calm. The place started filling up with elegant men and women. They took their places around the black tables as if they were extras from a New York film. The window reflected the stabs of time marked on my face. I was telling myself, I'll never forgive her, when a tall Texan imposed himself on me, asking if I knew how many miles per hour the wind was blowing.

"I haven't the slightest idea," I answered sharply.

I better leave, I said to myself. I tried to keep my balance and walk out gracefully.

The elevator door opened to a pair of solid Bostonian shoes and two very ladylike *zapatillas de charol*, shiny stiletto heels. I pressed the button to the twenty-first floor. A heavy key was hanging from the keyhole. As I turned it quietly, I heard a scream from inside. Genovesa had forgotten the key in the lock.

She saw the yellow shopping bag and asked me, in conciliatory tones, if I had bought any books. Once she realized I

79

wasn't going to answer, she confessed that she had gone looking for me in the museum.

She said she had left right away when she didn't find me. "Without you there was no sense in being there," she trailed off in a broken voice. "I decided I would wait here."

I flung myself onto the bed. I noticed the purple light that came in through our window every night. I closed my eyes to keep from feeling I was being observed.

Humming winds coiled like lace around the buildings' sharp tips. Genovesa suggested we go out for dinner, forget everything. Not a word came out of my pursed lips.

"We can't let the bad feelings get a hold on us and rot everything."

She spoke in all possible tones, from warm to desperate. In the end she threatened me. Pointing to the door, she said that if she crossed the threshold, I wouldn't see her again. She looked a hundred years old. I had an impulse to stop her but I couldn't move out of bed. She waited for an answer, and when she saw there wouldn't be any, she left, slamming the door.

The elevator goes tumbling down, a drop falls in the bathtub: splin, splash, splin; very near, a screw coils around its axis, cruaj, splin, splash, splin: the drop, the screw, the bolt, the elevator, the screw, the drop: phase one. Second phase: the drop, splin, splash, cruaj: my teeth demolish a cracker left over from breakfast, it sticks to my larynx. A raft of machine-gun fire penetrates my senses. I slam the TV set and turn it off.

After what seemed an eternity, Genovesa came back to the room. She was terribly pale; she turned to the wall and cried.

I wanted to hold her but my muscles wouldn't obey. I felt such anguish I was certain my brain would explode in a million pieces. Genovesa came close to me.

"Our relationship has never been easy," she said, touching my face.

I cried out like a wounded animal.

CLICKS

The following day we were walking on Avenue A. Bright colors—reds, yellows and blues: click. Thousands of words shamelessly advertising consumer products on the walls: click. New York's cruel face. Two Black men overdosing on heroin, unable to overcome fatigue: click. Anglo-Saxons and Puerto Ricans brushing each other's skins: click. Pale Genovesa: click.

"We must be crazy to be here. You know what they told us—not even the police come to this neighborhood," she whispered.

The intense yellow on the walls, the peculiar reds, the sky's distinct blues: click. Thousands of second and third-hand goods displayed on the sidewalk: click, click. Indecipherable tools, heterogeneous dwellers: click, click, click. A huge Coca-Cola sign: click. An appalling image: two expectant children facing torn walls and broken windows: click.

A man pops up from behind pressing something to my ribs. "I have a bottle in my house. You can take pictures of me there and suck my dick...you motherfuckers!"

"Let's get out of here!" Genovesa pleads.

I open the camera and yell in despair. "No! I didn't put the film in!"

"Check again, how can it be possible?"

"No, it's true. I'm an imbecile!"

"Calm down. We'll start all over again."

She walks a few steps away from me: click. The yellow wall, click, the bright letters, click, the amoral grafitti.

Every God-forsaken person on the street, click; Genovesa with tired eyes, click.

Just yesterday we were... "I'm sorry. I love you." Click. "I love you...."

From our bedroom window we watch the snow-covered roofs of the Metropolitan Museum. Genovesa comes naked towards the bed: click.

"Please, no more photographs."

"Yes, yes, please. You're beautiful. I love you, I want you…" Click.

BLOOD TESTS

Fate had plotted harsh tests for us when we arrived from New York, the kind I call blood tests.

On the morning of our arrival Genovesa went back to work at her studio. She called me on the phone a few hours later. "You'll never guess who's in México," she declared.

"Marta," I said without hesitation.

"*Eres bruja*, are you a witch, or what?" she asked in awe.

Marta was Morena's best friend in Paris, the one she wanted to help get off heroin.

Genovesa made plans to meet her at the Corinto Hotel, near Frontón México, that evening.

On the way, she warned me not to mention our relationship to Marta. "You mean that we're lovers?" I asked, annoyed.

"I don't want Morena to know," she explained, and kissed me to soften my discomfort.

While we were waiting in the lobby, a very beautiful young woman came out of the elevator. She walked absently, her eyes set on the worn-out rug at her feet.

"Perhaps it isn't her," I whispered.

Genovesa walked over and made her stop abruptly. "Are you Marta?"

They started a conversation as if they had known each other for years. I had to introduce myself. Marta stared at me as if trying to find a clue to my identity in an archive of myriad memories. "Oh yes, Morena's friend," she said at last.

"That's me," I smiled.

We sat down on the only sofa in the lobby, three in a row. *La bella* was deathly pale. She explained that she had come to México for the same reasons Morena came.

"You're here on a cure?" I inquired.

"Yes I am."

There was nothing to hide once the worst had been said. She got up and announced she was awfully thirsty. She asked if we could take her for an orange juice someplace. Genovesa wanted a cup of coffee, so I decided to drive to the Colonia Roma and show Marta our impoverished little Europe. As we drove, I noticed nothing seemed to attract our visitor's attention.

At the café Bella Italia, she ordered a huge orange juice and drank it in one gulp. Then she told us she had come to México with her father and his mistress. Recently she had lived through a frightful experience and had decided that the trip was her only chance to stay alive. Joao, her seven-year-old son, had found her lying unconscious on the bathroom floor. She had almost died from an overdose. The boy, terrified, had run to a neighbor. The neighbor had called Marta's mother and she got Marta into the hospital.

"All this happened while I was still in a coma. But once inside the hospital the worst of ordeals began. They were all such clean and moral people...God!...and all those Christs hanging from white walls."

She let her head drop back and a grimace of pain showed on her face. "I'm so thirsty!" she interrupted herself, and ordered another orange juice. "I swore I'd get off the drug forever," she added, and her eyes filled with tears. "My son has no reason to suffer; it's for his sake I want to get cured."

Genovesa took Marta's hand in hers. "I'm sure it's the right decision," she said reassuringly.

Marta went on to tell us how she had met Joao's father.

"He was an upper-class guy from Barcelona," she said, looking out of the window. "The bastard got me into drugs and once we were both up to our necks he just split."

Marta ordered a scoop of coffee ice cream. After she had finished it she talked like a different person. She said she couldn't understand how she had been pumping such deadly powder into her body. "You can die, you know. Puf! just like that," she snapped her fingers, "and without even knowing it."

I prompted her to change the subject; it was clearly too painful.

Little by little, she began to relax and her beauty surfaced. She talked about her work. The documentary she had written and directed had won a prize in France. She was very proud of it.

"Everything seemed to be working out well then but, as they say, life is a wheel of fortune, no doubt."

She looked at her watch. She had to leave. Her father would be taking her out for dinner to some chic place. This made her laugh at last.

"I've got to tell you something. I'm going to Acapulco tomorrow and I'm terribly worried. I have needle marks all over and if I put on a bathing suit, I'm sure they'll notice."

We tried to convince her to stay in the city instead. She became noticeably anxious, claiming that her father wouldn't understand.

Genovesa had been quiet a long time. I knew something was gnawing at her; that Morena was a source of worry. She couldn't miss this opportunity to ask Marta about her.

"Oh, she's fine, just fine," Marta replied, trying to smile. Genovesa gave me a wise look. Later, when we were alone, she insisted that Marta was lying. Her face paled as she considered the possibility that her cousin was in a situation similar to Marta's. I hadn't seen her so gloomy in a long time.

Marta called at seven the next morning to say she had finally managed to find a place to stay in México. A friend of hers, the Diva of Vienna, would be taking her in for a few days. We promised to visit her that evening.

MORENA'S FRIEND

We found the house on the old road to Cuernavaca. We rang the buzzer several times but no one came to the door. Through a slat in the doorway, we peeped in at the unlit mansion. We rang insistently. Ten minutes later there was still no answer.

"Marta is there," Genovesa claimed.

"Get down on your knees and mesh your fingers," I ordered. "You'll be my springboard." Lifting my boot, I stepped on the improvised ladder and climbed the fence. From there I leapt down like a cat.

"Bravo!" she cried as I unlocked the gate for her. We walked apprehensively across a huge, deserted garden. All the windows in the house were covered with thick blankets to protect the inside.

Suddenly we heard a noise somewhere in back of us. Genovesa screamed in terror. I turned to look for the ghost. A huge black cat with yellow eyes was staring at us.

"It climbed the gate but without the help of your fingers," I whispered, amused. We laughed until we were in tears.

We circled the house and found an apartment of sorts in the back. A dying light filtered through its half-closed door. Genovesa grabbed my hand and begged that we get out of there immediately. Her reaction made me chuckle.

"Don't laugh!" she demanded with a serious face.

The hinges shrieked. She followed behind me, on tiptoe, across a dimly lit hallway towards a cold, dark room. A naked dummy, held by strings, hung from the ceiling; there was a double bed underneath it.

Marta was sitting on a rickety chair with her feet resting on a hulk that had once been a heater. She didn't notice our arrival. She might be dead for all we know, I thought, horrified.

Genovesa walked over and stroked her hair. Marta sat in a deep stupor; she slowly looked up but didn't recognize Genovesa. I was watching the scene so intently that I tripped over a cardboard box. The noise frightened her. She jumped up and shouted, "Stop, stop, Joao! Watch out for the cars, they're rushing by so fast. Be careful!"

I ran to her side and grabbed her arm to stop her. "Your boy is in Paris, remember? He's staying at your mother's."

She stared at me as though she were coming out of the darkness, then sat back down and began to cry painfully. It was terrible to see such a young woman so torn apart.

Her friend and hostess had given her the number of a health clinic in the neighborhood. "In case of an emergency," she had said before she left for work. Marta told us she had been feeling worse and worse as the day went on. "Withdrawal symptoms," she said. At dusk she had decided that she needed some sedatives and had gone over to the clinic. The doctor who looked her over had tried to rape her. "The swine! He tried to force me," she cried. Then she sank back into her previous torpor.

I decided to call a dear friend of mine, a psychoanalyst, to ask his advice. He said he was in the middle of a dinner party but promised to come as soon as possible. Genovesa and I sighed with relief.

When he arrived he talked with Marta in private for a long time. Afterwards he told us that her use of drugs was connected with her continual solitude.

"She probably has the drug with her and I don't think it's wise that she be left alone," he advised.

Genovesa called her grandmother for help. The old woman said she would take care of Morena's friend. "Bring her over to the house, she can stay here."

She looked patiently after Marta for a week. She said she couldn't understand how a pretty girl like that could be depressed all the time.

When she was well enough to take the plane back to Paris, we drove her to the airport. Before saying goodbye at the gate, she called Genovesa aside. "Morena needs help and quickly," she warned. Then she walked away with her sad, weary stride.

A DEEP VOYAGE
INTO THE
PHILOSOPHICAL MATRIX

It was seven in the morning. Our airplane cleaved through the amber layer of the Mexican sky; it climbed up with a noteworthy effort. Genovesa closed her eyes and held my hand. A change in the cabin's pressure forced her to open them again.

Little by little, the sky turned blue until it glowed. Far in the distance, two solitary peaks with snow on their tips, Popocatépetl and La Mujer Dormida, the Sleeping Woman, were watching the future pass by. Underneath us lay a mattress of white clouds like the sea.

"Hallucinatory," Genovesa noted, observing the breathtaking scenery.

The sun lit up her face. I kissed her, unaware of anything else, until I heard the stewardess approaching. She stared at us and asked if we wanted a cup of coffee.

"For me, a *tequila doble*, please."

"This early?" Genovesa asked. "Okay, then give me a glass of white wine."

"To the ocean, to love," we toasted.

Three sea gulls came gliding into view: Puerto Vallarta was within sight.

We didn't leave the hotel room until nightfall. The sky was overcast. The waiter told us that Norma, the tornado, was coming into shore. All through the night we listened to the wind howling. The sounds made an impact on our urban senses. The storm was wild and unrelenting, but after making love, we forgot the winds and fell asleep in each other's arms.

The next day, a heedless bluster untied the ocean's fury. Genovesa wanted to go down to the docks. She sat on the planks' edge and stared at the open sea.

Far in the distance we could hear the whistle of a ship. I wrote its name in my journal—*Bagatella,* the freighter. Vignettes of smoke drifted from its chimney. I imagined two women on their way to the Orient, standing beside their trunks on the prow.

Genovesa had become distant. Stormy waves were pounding against the rocks at the bottom of the palisade. Nailed to the perpetual noise, I remembered the passion we had shared during the night: the room, our skins. Desire always renewing itself, without fail, without limits. Hurt by the shift in her mood, I filled my mind with naval routes. My gaze was struck by a pelican resting on the stormy waters. It had a notorious fluorescent eye.

Genovesa noticed I had withdrawn. She touched my arm as if she hadn't meant to. I saw her out of the corner of my eye; two tears were falling down her cheeks. I caressed her face burdened with pain. She was afraid she wouldn't be in time to save Morena. With a tired look, she asked me to walk along the beach with her. The prints of our naked feet sank into the wet sand; the sea erased them.

"On days like this, it all seems so futile," she told me. We talked about death. Our somber spirits filled the air. She stared at the horizon.

"I want to make love to you," she said all of a sudden. There was light in her eyes. I was surprised by her unexpected desire.

"And I want you to make love to me."

We kissed on the silvery beach, then ran across the street without thinking about cars. A bus sped past, whistling in our ears. We stopped, breathless, in front of the torn ocher facade of the Hotel Pacífico and hugged each other.

For a long time, we stood on the balcony embracing. When we went into the room the clocks of the world stopped.

When I woke up the next morning, Genovesa was not at my side. I wondered if she could have left me and I was filled with anguish. I bolted out of bed and peeked out the door of the balcony. There she was, standing with the white shawl around her shoulders, looking at the lighthouse. Her hair was blowing, guided by the sea winds. A lightning bolt sizzled across the sky like a serpent of fire. Genovesa moved her hands along her waist and pressed her belly. She sensed she was being observed so I went to her and planted a kiss on her cheek. She turned to my mouth with a strong new passion. I wrapped my hands around her waist and felt her breath stirring in my ear. She kissed my neck. I slipped my hands inside her shawl and touched her cold breasts, her hard nipples. Standing on tiptoe, she passed her tongue over my lips, my cheeks, my neck. She went down on my breasts; she bit one nipple softly, then the other. In the distance, the lighthouse flashed. I grabbed her hair and pulled her to my mouth.

"I want to make love to you," I said.

"I *want* you to make love to me," she answered, clinging to my body like a wet sail to its mast.

When we left the room again, the clocks began to count the time. I felt as if my life was only now beginning.

RECKLESS MIND

We came back to México City with premonitions of disaster. It was midnight; the moon clung to dense black clouds. Our reckless thoughts ceased. I clutched at her body. Two longish shadows undulated in the bedroom mirrors. Genovesa turned to look at the darkness outside. The weeping willows were whispering wind sounds. The pleasure on her face lost its texture and gave way to infinite traces of pain. She was leaving for Paris and this could mean we wouldn't be seeing each other again. We were both aware of her unspoken wish to flee from our love affair.

"I'll be back, I love you," she said as if reading my thoughts. She gave me a long kiss that unravelled other kisses.

We fell asleep as the birds' warble announced the morning. A while later, Genovesa got up to take care of the last details before her trip. Then she asked me to go out on the terrace with her. I knew she wanted to etch in her memory the place where we had been happy so many times. She thoughtfully contemplated the space that had been our witness.

"Isn't it true they blossom the whole year round?" she asked pointing to the flowers and forcing a smile. We kissed as if we wanted to steal each other's soul. She didn't want to leave and I didn't want her to leave. But she had to.

We silently got into the black Mustafá. I put on my dark glasses and turned on the engine. She put in the tape she had recorded the night before and flicked the deck on. My music, which had seemed *demodé* to her when we first met, was now our music.

She said it would keep her company in Paris.

"Sur les plages blanches deux amantes se font l'amour," Barriére's sweet voice sang.

91

On Churubusco Avenue, the SAHOP, the Public Construction Department, asked to be forgiven for the trouble it was causing. We were forced to take a long detour, so it wasn't easy to be gracious.

Genovesa didn't take her eyes off my mouth during the whole drive. I knew she wanted me but she had to act with restraint now. When I turned to her, she covered her mouth with the palm of her hand. I grabbed her hand and we quickly kissed with tears in our eyes.

Cosmic forces joined together to help me find the perfect parking space. The security guards at the doors let me follow her into the Air France terminal where only passengers with boarding passes could enter.

"Lovers' luck," she said, looking at me fixedly. Mexican music was streaming out of the plane's open door. We hugged and kissed goodbye in front of an astonished stewardess.

Genovesa walked through the heavy metal door and turned to look at me for the last time. The music stopped.

Right on schedule, the silver paradox lifted from the ground.

As I drove back home with a sad soul, I made up my mind to write the story of two women: Valeria and Genovesa.

II

MY HOUSE

The bed moved up and down, creaking. He groaned. Ssh! be quiet. Stone silence. My mother rocked my crib with her foot. Then, the moan of a wounded animal echoed through the house. My mother left the bedroom to go to the bathroom; she flushed the toilet. When she came back he was already snoring. She kept rocking my crib with her foot until she fell asleep. I don't remember if I was three months or three years old.

My father used to wake up early. He would go to the window and look out at the gloomy patio downstairs. He would caress the lank hairs of his armpit and stretch, roaring like a lion. Putting on the same clothes he'd strewn on the chair the night before, he would leave the house without saying goodbye to anyone. My mother said he went to work for us.

He was not aware of the blue sky as he walked to the little store where he sold construction materials. He had only one idea fixed in his mind: to become rich. A deep scar on his left cheek, stamped by the kick of a horse, gave him a peculiar look. He had been wounded in Russia when he was seven; his mother had died a few months later. My father never forgave her for that. When he got angry the scar trembled, and then we would all tremble.

He came back late at night. Stiff-kneed, he would head for the huge brown radio on top of the chest and turn it on: "You are now listening to XEW de México." The people they talked about were always the same: Hitler, Mussolini, Roosevelt, Stalin, Churchill, the Pope Pio XII.

It was while we were listening that he told me we had family in Europe, my grandmother's mother, her sisters and several cousins. My grandmother wept when she thought of them; she said they were in great danger. "We are lucky to have left Europe," my mother would say, thanking the Lord.

95

Then the Americans entered the war. That came as good news to my father. Some time later, we heard on the same brown radio that the war was over. My parents embraced each other and danced; my grandmother wouldn't stop crying. My father opened a bottle of whisky and offered her a drink. After a while she was dancing too.

During that period we started building our new house, designed as an exact replica of the Cine Metropolitan, a movie house my mother liked very much. According to my grandmother it would be like a palace. But the construction was going very slowly. Changes and more changes were made to the color until the blue, pink and beige cornices matched the original perfectly.

Hidden behind the curtains of our downtown apartment, I watched the neighborhood boys playing ball for the last time. My mother and Lucía were putting the last few things in cardboard boxes. When there was nothing else to pack, we put the boxes inside the light blue Chrysler with the little winged horse on its hood.

We left under the wings of pigeons that had come to drink from the fountain of San Jacinto. My mother told us not to look back because it was bad luck. No one did.

We took possession of our castle in *la colonia* Anzures when the Anzures was still an empty plain. I now had a room to myself. A week after we moved I turned five years old.

Soon after our move we learned that aunts, cousins and my great grandmother had been gassed in Hitler's ovens. The Movietone newsreels showed children who looked like starved birds; the images wouldn't let me sleep at night. My mother told me I had a long life ahead of me to forget these horrors. But I never did.

Little by little, fine porcelains and heavy bronzes began crowding into our castle. There, my destiny was defined: to be silent, always silent. My mother had set opinions about everything and she wouldn't be contradicted. Drowned in his business, my father only used his voice to give orders. Thus, keeping quiet, I lost the art of speech.

The house deeply inspired the production of my dreams. I dreamed obsessively of uninvented spaces: of another house in the basement of our castle. In the beginning I was afraid to walk around by myself. But later, I could always find a room with a glowing fireplace where people were gathered. Someone would come over and greet me warmly. They would ask me how I was feeling and what I was thinking. I spent many joyful moments there among people with whom I could talk.

THE GHOST

The door cracked open. A ghost came in; walked one, two, three steps; click, set the glass of hot cocoa on the bedside table. It went to the window, drew the curtains, pulled the blinds half open. Myself, not exactly Lady Godiva, with traces of insomnia and bad breath, turned my head to the wall.

Lucía knelt next to my bed. "Take your foot out," she ordered. She slipped on one white knee-sock, then the other, and pulled the navy blue uniform over my head. Lastly, she put my sweater on. Ouch, it scratched.

"Drink it," she said.

"Drink what?"

"Don't be silly, you know what." Lucía had yellow eyes and a long black braid that hung down on her electric-blue sweater. She never smiled and only obeyed my mother's orders.

When she left the room, I jumped back into bed. Lying in front of the tall oyster-colored wardrobe, I pressed my fingertips to my eyes to watch, as I opened them, ay! how the huge thing started falling on top of me.

Aj! I imagined the eggs' grease floating in the cocoa.

I began to worry that it was getting late so I left my room and found the bathroom door closed; my brother was still inside. I knocked on the door quietly. I didn't want to wake up my parents; they had a very active social life. I knocked again.

When my brother came out he looked at me from head to toe and called me *pendeja*, as he did every morning. *Puto*, I thought to myself, but said nothing or I would get my face slapped.

I dipped my fingertips in the warm water of the bathroom sink and wiped my eyes. I spread Colgate on my toothbrush, put it into my mouth and with my free hand poured the cocoa down the sink. I let the hot water run until every drop of grease vanished.

Just then, Lucía came running in to pick up my school pack. The bus was already waiting outside. Mario, the driver, didn't honk the horn in the mornings like he did at other children's homes. It was my mother's request and my mother always got her way because she was beautiful.

"Such a lazy girl, *huevona, huevonzota,*" Mario said as I climbed into the bus. Sometimes he'd say *huevoncita,* his tone sweet or threatening according to his mood.

Just before I reached my seat, he stepped on the gas and my tender butt crashed on the hard wooden bench. He smiled at me through the rearview mirror, showing his white teeth. I smiled too, motioning that I would pay him back for that.

The bus route was long. After picking me and my brother up, Mario went to pick up Chabela and her two small brothers. They were red-headed twins with freckles all over their faces. Chabela always climbed on with a petulant look on her face; she would smooth the pleats on her skirt and sit on her fat butt. She was the best student in class, that's why she thought she was so special.

Mario was late again; he rushed, as always, to get to school in time. I loved speed and he knew it. As we were driving past the school's red gate I shut my mouth so I wouldn't bite my tongue and waited for the bus to go over the street bump. Right at that moment the school bell rang.

Prefecto Alba blew his whistle and we all ran to stand in line.

The principal, who had just arrived from a concentration camp, recently liberated at the end of the war, stood very still next to the flagpoles and waited until everything was so quiet you could hear the buzzing of a fly.

"Silence!" he cried in his newly learned Spanish. "We will sing the hymns: the Mexican first and then the Israeli."

We finally had our own state now and nobody could kill me as they had killed my cousins. My grandmother had just received word that all her sisters had been murdered by the Nazis. A survivor from her small town in Lithuania had brought the news. He told her that her cousin Abraham had miraculously escaped to Israel and had asked him to look for her when he came to México.

As we sang, I recalled how my father had brought home the first Israeli calendar some days ago. My mother had hung it on the dining room wall. It had a picture of strong, sun tanned girls working on the land. They smiled happily and I regretted that I didn't look like them.

Lost in thought, I noticed that Chabela was gossiping with Ana and pointing at me. What was she telling her? They both laughed. Oh, how I hated them!

The principal ordered us to our classrooms.

The first hour was devoted to prayer and the study of religion. Mr. Morningstar told us to open our Bibles and read the morning psalms.

"The day of atonement is near," the teacher said. "It's the day when God decides who's going to live and who's going to die. This decision depends on our behavior during the year."

My father was of the opinion that all those beliefs were *pendejadas;* who better than him to know, since his father had been a rabbi? We used to drive on Shabbat, for instance, and we hadn't died.

Someone in the back laughed. Morningstar turned to face the class and yelled, "Who was it?" Nobody answered. He asked again, straining his voice. He walked to the back of the room, grabbed Schatz by his sweater and pulled him to the raised platform up front. Poor Schatz swore he didn't do it; he claimed it was Max who had laughed. Max emitted a rat-like shriek, saying it wasn't true. The teacher ordered Schatz to raise his arms and hold the heavy wooden basket on top of his head.

"Don't move until it's time for recess," he cried. "And now we shall continue with Yom Kippur, the day of forgiveness."

When the bell for recess rang, I waited for everyone to leave the room. I went into the empty kindergarten grounds and hid in the gray grass that thrived along the wire fence. Now I was able to see without being seen.

The children resembled colonies of bacteria coming together and breaking apart. Chabela and Ana were jumping rope. I wanted to jump too; I had never done it before. I looked into the paper bag at the *tortas* that Lucía had given me before leaving the house. When I was certain nobody was watching, I dumped everything into the trash can and before I even knew how, I was jumping rope. Then Chabela tightened the cord and I fell on my hands, barely saving my teeth. With a sly smile, I went and punched her nose; it started bleeding immediately. Oy, God, I'm in trouble now, I thought. She rushed into the girls' bathroom and Ana trailed behind.

The bell for Spanish class rang. Professor Méndez was wiping the hieroglyphs that Lerer Morningstar had left on the blackboard. He cleaned the white dust from his hands with a gesture of annoyance. He opened the green arithmetic book and said we were very behind in divisions. He ordered us to sit and copy in our notebooks the series of divisions he would write on the blackboard. Chabela hadn't come back by the time he had finished. Oy, I moaned, she surely went to tell the principal and he must be calling my mother right now. Just then Chabela walked in with swollen red eyes and blood clotted around her nose. Méndez didn't ask her a thing. Of course not; she was the best in class.

León, who sat behind me, nudged me on the shoulder. He handed me a piece of paper with a hundred folds. Surely it was Chabela, passing on her news. We were still working on the divisions and Méndez was pacing down the rows. I unfolded the note. I love you, it said. Pier had signed it. He must be making fun of me, I thought, and turned to look at him; he smiled and winked. He was certainly the best-looking guy in class. I became his *novia,* his sweetheart that same day. That made me equal to the rest of the girls, Chabela included.

I was soon aware that a third party was involved: Chucho, the son of the driver of bus number 4. Chucho stood guard outside the bathroom door when Pier and I kissed for the first time. He also kept an eye out when I pulled my panties down and Pier touched me with his little thing.

Chucho wanted to know what it felt like. Pier told him it was delicious. I kept quiet because girls weren't supposed to speak about these things.

He'll have to find someone else to show him, I thought. But he threatened that he would tell my brother everything. Chucho won.

I soon became the most popular girl in school, even with the older boys. I always knew what they wanted....

WRESTLING MATCH

It was Friday, the last day of school. My mother announced we were going to the movies after lunch. The film, with Stewart Granger and Ava Gardner, was playing at Cine Variedades. My mother liked them both, but especially Ava because she was said to resemble her.

When the meal was over and my parents left the table, my brother smeared his hands with chicken grease, came over and wiped them on my head. I wanted to scream at the top of my lungs but I restrained myself. I didn't want my mother to say I was a pansy and then not take me to the movies.

The film took place in Africa. I thought it was nice, but Mother didn't like it. She said she couldn't relate to those faraway places. Now I wasn't sure if I had liked it or not.

As we came out into the street, she told me that she and my father were going to dinner with the Americans. Kuntz and Morton weren't really American, they were Scottish, and my mother thought they drank too much. She worried that my father would take on their habits but she always forgave them because, after all, they appreciated her female beauty.

"They were the ones who lent your father his first cement sack when he was still a nobody," she repeated for the hundredth time. Now my father owned the largest *cementera* in México and I should be proud of him.

For a moment I fantasized that dinner would spare me from our customary after-movie walk.

Ah, but mother adored her walks. She clasped my hand and pulled me next to her. I had to stride at her pace and never turn to look around. She was the queen and I the little princess.

We reached Zapatería del Prado. There she stopped; shoes were her weakness. She finally let go of my hand and I was free to watch the people passing by. She was tempted to walk into the store but it was late. So she took my hand once more and off we went, rushing until we reached Cinco de Mayo Street where she had parked the car.

When we arrived home, she went up to her room to get ready.

My brother and I sat with the TV on. "The Nescafé Show" with Pedro Vargas, Verónica Loyo and the comedians Manolín and Chilinsky was starting.

Mother walked downstairs with her evening stride. We looked at her in admiration. She asked what we wanted for supper. *"Taquitos de pollo, quesadillas o enchiladas verdes?"*

I wanted *enchiladas* and my brother wanted that too, plus a steak, *frijolitos,* and ah, *un bolillo,* a piece of bread. He's such a pig, I thought.

When mother left the room to get Lucía to prepare dinner, Efraín said to me, "You filthy pig!"

So I was the pig? I didn't understand a thing.

"Just wait until they leave and you'll see," he threatened.

Father came in from work. He walked up the front steps in twos and mumbling "hello," disappeared upstairs to take a shower. Ten minutes later he was downstairs again, holding the cuff on his left wrist. Mother buttoned his cuff link, muttering, "You good-for-nothing, do you have two left hands or what?"

I thought they looked like movie stars. I didn't want them to leave; I didn't want to stay alone with my brother. Mother told us to go to bed when the *Lucha Libre,* the wrestling matches were over. Immediately after we heard the wheels shriek around the corner of Gutenberg, Efraín was on top of me. He grabbed my hands and pulled me up; he twisted my arm around my back in a *manita de puerco.*

"Tell me, you whore! *A ver puta!* What do you do with the boys in the school bathroom?" My heart stopped. "It's none of your business," I yelled. He pressed my hand harder, forcing me to kneel down. I screamed; I was sure he would break it. Lucía called in from the kitchen to ask something about his supper. He let go to answer.

I concentrated on the TV screen so he wouldn't notice I was shaking, when suddenly ay! a bucket of cold water ran down my spine. "You bastard!" I yelled.

"All the way from Arena Coliseo: *Máscara contra Cabellera*. El Cavernario Galindo and Wolf Ruvinskis against El Santo and Blue Demon." The wrestling matches were about to start.

I went up to my bedroom to change clothes. Upstairs, I had a brilliant idea. I tiptoed into my parents' bedroom and seized the water pitcher. I stood holding fast to the handrail and emptied the pitcher on my brother as if he were a plant. The whole house echoed with my loud laughter. He came running upstairs so fast that for a moment I thought he was skinny instead of fat. He twisted my hand again and forced me to fill the pitcher from the bathroom faucet. After I did, I managed to pull away from his grip.

I rushed into the kitchen, breathless, hoping that Lucía would save me. Lucía wasn't there. I went into the dining room; my brother was already waiting for me and we circled around the table, hitting the glass cabinet where my mother kept her fine china. Suddenly, Efraín made a false turn and crish, crash, crunch. I approached cautiously to see what had happened. Ay, his hand was bleeding profusely. I wanted to say something but he grabbed my foot, whirled me to the floor, put his knees over my arms and jumped on them with his whole weight. He slapped me in the face and smashed his fist into my collarbone.

I kicked with no results. He's going to kill me, I thought.

"Help!" I screamed. "Help!"

Lucía walked in calmly and told him to leave me alone. He struck another blow to my face as if he hadn't heard. "If you don't let her go, I'll tell your mother, tomorrow."

"Tomorrow? Tomorrow, it's me who's going to tell on this whore," he yelled.

He stood up, raving, and walked out licking his bloody hand.

THE BEATING

On Sunday we didn't leave our rooms until Grandmother called to ask what time we would pick her up. We could hear my mother crossing the hallway like a soldier. In a long flowered bathrobe, she stood by the door that separated my brother's room from mine. With her face half made-up, she said it was already late. She turned to look at me. "Put on your new dress, and hurry because we're not going to wait for you. Do you hear?"

"Yes," I answered.

My mother went back to her room. My brother hadn't opened his mouth. Perhaps he forgave me, I thought, but then I heard his door slam. Oh, how I wished I could stop being afraid.

My father came to take a shower in the big bathroom. My parents had bought a safebox a month before and hidden it under their own shower floor. So now we all used the big bathroom. I imagined the water running down my father's body and shivered.

I went to the window to look at the empty lots of La Anzures. Everything was calm and quiet. My father came out of the bathroom and yelled to my brother that he could go in now. Meanwhile, I put on the new dress my mother had made to order from the Spanish ladies of Cinco de Mayo Street. It was yellow with green trim. I looked horrible, but according to her, it complemented my black hair. I was nervous and I was late again. My mother didn't stop honking the horn until she saw me standing in front of the car. I climbed inside next to my brother Efraín, who moved over so I wouldn't touch him.

"It's like silk," my mother said, referring to the smooth way our new white Cadillac convertible ran. Everybody stared at it; there was one other like it in México.

My father took Gutenberg Avenue and went down Tíber Street at full speed. We circled the Parque México. My grandmother had moved there after her second husband had died. Now she spent alternate days with us and with her other daughter.

My father honked the horn. She thrust her head out the window and yelled, *"Voy!"* making it sound like *buey* or ox. This time nobody laughed at the way she mispronounced her Spanish. She walked through the glass door of the Edificio Basurto and climbed stiffly into the back of the two-door car. Uf! she had too much perfume on. My father started coughing and so did I. My mother turned to me and was about to snap her usual "Oh, don't be so delicate" when my grandmother interrupted in Yiddish, "Your car is beautiful, you should use it in good health."

My father thanked her, also in Yiddish, and asked my mother where we should head for lunch. Those things she decided.

"To the Normandie, downtown," she answered. I was glad she chose such an elegant place because my brother wouldn't be able to say anything there.

My father showed off his El Dorado by driving it at full speed; my grandmother smiled approvingly. On López Street he turned left.

Holding the red velvet handrail, we descended the stairs, one after the other. The restaurant was packed. My mother, looking straight ahead of her, followed the captain; my grandmother did the same.

People stared at us, but we weren't supposed to look back. Now it was my turn to walk proudly. I felt like I had swallowed a broomstick and my lips trembled. The captain left the black leather menus on the table but neither my mother, my grandmother, nor I opened them because we already knew what we wanted. My father and brother took a while to decide. The maitre d' said that meanwhile he would bring the drinks. My brother seized this opportunity to say he had something very important to tell them. I wanted to beg him, please, not to do it. It would be my death.

"She," he said, pointing at me, "goes into the school's bathroom and does filthy things with the older boys."

"Filthy things? What do you mean, filthy things?" asked my mother.

The scar on my father's left cheek trembled. Without saying a word he took out his wallet and threw a wad of bills on the table top.

"Let's go!" he ordered in a hoarse voice.

Nobody spoke a word while we drove back. I wanted to ask someone to help me, but nobody would. When we got home, my father stepped out of the car with his belt ready in his hand. My mother yelled at him not to do it on the street. "The neighbors might see." It was too late: my father was already hitting me with his belt buckle. He chased me along the stairs. The blows fell on my back, my buttocks, my legs; he hit me on the head. I ran to the bathroom and tried to hide in the bathtub. My father followed me, my mother behind him. The belt sizzled like a whip. "Whore," my father was screaming, sweating heavily. I always knew I would die very young. I had no strength left to moan when my father hurled the belt away and left the bathroom.

My grandmother came in and told my mother that was no way to treat a child. My mother yelled at her to shut up and leave the bathroom immediately. She obeyed, shaking her head. My mother sat on the edge of the tub. She took my burning hand that lay limply on my belly.

"If you had come to me and told me everything," she said, "this wouldn't have happened. I'm your mother, you should have told me."

I pulled my hand away. In a broken voice I told her that my brother was such a tattletale. She claimed he had done it for my own good. I don't know how I found the strength to yell at her, "Get out and leave me alone." She slammed the door proudly and went to the bedroom to join her husband.

Everything hurt and a polar coldness ran through my entire body. I got out of the bathtub and stood near the window. There was peace in the world outside. I turned my eyes to the sky and asked God to kill me. "Kill me, please God, kill me," I repeated untiringly. I waited hours for my prayer to be heard, but nothing happened. He didn't listen.

I heard my parents' bedroom door open. I'm sure they have an appointment for dinner, I thought bitterly. I ran to my bed and shut my eyes.

After they had left, I put my hand to my clitoris. I felt nothing....

107

INSOMNIA

I was delirious; the high fever was calcifying my brain. Neither teas nor aspirins did any good. Desperately, my mother continued to try to reach Doctor Cedillo at his house; time after time no one answered. "I'm sure he left his phone unplugged," she fumed.

It was dawn when he finally answered the phone. He said there was an epidemic in México; he had to attend to an emergency case first and then he would come see me. My mother insisted that her daughter's case was urgent too. She begged him to come see me first, but she couldn't persuade him.

Cedillo arrived a few minutes before noon. He came into my bedroom followed by his enormous hump. His appearance frightened me. He put his shiny black bag on the chest of drawers and took out a few things. His checkup was thorough: reflexes, lungs, heart, stomach. Taking good care not to dishevel his hair, he placed his little lamp around his head and introduced his hairy hands into my throat. "Repeat: aga, aga." After poking deeply, he dumped the wooden stick in the trash bin my mother offered. His hands, as he rubbed them together, made a dry little noise. He said, "Diphtheria, my dear lady. That's what I feared it would be."

With a white face, my mother jumped off the chair. "Will she die?"

"Oh no, my dear lady," he burst out laughing. "With penicillin, nobody dies these days. But there are exceptions. This morning, for instance, before coming here, I visited a boy with the same illness as your daughter's. The poor child was black and blue and I had to perform a tracheotomy." He turned his head to look at me. "Yes, about her same age."

"Tracheotomy? What does that mean?" I asked. Cedillo slid a finger across his throat as if it were a sharp knife. "A slit for air to go in," he replied.

Suddenly I couldn't breathe and I tossed and turned in bed desperately. My mother, on the other hand, had calmed down completely. She crossed her legs and got ready for an amiable chat with the little man.

Lost in worry, I couldn't figure out why Doctor Cedillo, with a smile hidden under his mustache a la Dalí, was talking about a tunnel, a secret tunnel…. "If lovers could be confident that no one would see them, they would certainly be waiting in line…ha ha ha," he laughed.

My mother pointed at me to remind him he should watch his words.

"Oh, it's better they learn about life when they're young," he said without looking at me.

At which my mother claimed, "Perhaps mankind won't know, but you can't hide anything from God."

Doctor Cedillo turned on his seat. "God, my dear lady, has too many things to do to worry about such nonsense…ha ha ha."

"Don't be so sure, Doctor. My mother, who's a wise woman, always said, 'Sins you commit, your children will pay for.'"

"Well, well…it's time to go back to work," he said, getting on his feet. My mother, with a nice smile, followed him to the door.

Children will pay…bah! That's really too much, I thought as I listened to them walking down the stairs. That night I couldn't sleep. Every time I closed my eyes I saw my throat being cut.

YOM KIPPUR

Everyone quickly forgot that damned Sunday. Everyone except me. My mother was the worst of all. I would never forgive her for letting my father beat me so cruelly and, on top of that, saying that my brother had only wanted what was best for me.

The Day of Atonement arrived; we had to go to the synagogue and ask forgiveness from God. My brother complained that we shouldn't be driving the car on such a sacred day. "It's mortal sin," he muttered in his know-it-all voice. My father chuckled and my mother replied, "You wouldn't want us to walk all the way downtown, would you?" They both laughed, and I felt like laughing too.

My father checked the back seat to see if his phylacteries and yarmulke were there. We were already late and we still had to pick Grandmother up. At the synagogue she always sat by my mother.

My brother kept on annoying everybody. He said he would be a rabbi when he grew up. That really bothered my father; his scar trembled. His own father had done nothing but study the Bible while he and his brothers had starved. "You're crazy!" he yelled at my brother, and stepped on the gas, making us all fall back in our seats.

At the synagogue the women sat upstairs while the men stayed on the ground floor. Professor Morningstar told us that God preferred women to stay at home praying. When he said this, the children in class made up a little tune: "The women in the kitchen...while men go out to pray, pray, pray...."

Their silliness didn't get to me; I could sit downstairs with the men if I wanted to. My father never asked permission to do what he pleased and often he would just take me in. But this time, the idea of sitting next to him seemed unbearable. My mother took my hand and we climbed proudly up the stairs with Grandmother. I sat between them.

The principal's wife was gossiping with dentist Samuel's wife about us. My mother greeted the shrews with a nod; both smiled falsely and wished her a happy new year in unison.

At that very minute I remembered that I didn't believe in God anymore, but before I could finish the thought, I was already repentant.

My father, with his phylacteries strapped around his arms, turned his head to look for us. He set in place the white and gold-threaded yarmulke he had bought for Efraín's bar mitzvah. It was the first time my brother was fasting and he felt like such a grown-up already.

For some reason, I thought of my father's father, whom I had only seen once in a photograph. He was an old man with a long white beard and very sad little eyes; he died a few days before I was born. It occurred to me now that he had died to leave me his place in this world. My mother used to say he looked so old because he had seen his parents killed by a group of drunken Cossacks. "God, please kill our enemies," I prayed with all my heart. Then I heard the rabbi's voice rising in a frightful yell.

"Upstairs!" he said, shaking his hands and looking up to the sky. "The women are asked to be quiet. God, make them quiet!"

The other rabbi, the one with the goatee, announced it was time to say Kaddish for the dead. He asked the children and the people without dead to leave the house of God.

As I was walking downstairs I felt a tiny paper shot hit my buttock; I turned to look for the culprit. Pierre was standing on the stairs above me, smiling happily. I suddenly was afraid that my brother was watching me, so I rushed to hide under the stairwell. I waited there for the prayers to be over. Oh, they took forever.

Later, when a few of the grown-ups came out on the patio to rest from the fast, I went back to my place at my mother's side.

I saw Ishie, the synagogue keeper, standing near the cantor's pulpit. He brought a little snuffbox out of the pocket of his old jacket, held the tobacco under the nose of one of my schoolmates and waited for him to inhale. The boy sneezed: once, then a second time. Everyone laughed. Staring out of his little blue eyes, Ishie put the box back into his pocket and patted the boy's head.

I also liked to sneeze with Ishie's tobacco. I will never smell his snuffbox again, I said to myself sadly. I wondered if he ever left the synagogue. He might not even have known how the downtown streets looked. The idea seemed terrifying.

Life had changed so much since that Sunday.

BAD TIMES

It seemed as if the terrors of suffocation had wiped out my brain cells. I simply could not divide. The school principal called my mother to convey the sad fact. They decided I needed daily private lessons at home, plus my mother's help. Impossible. There was just no way to open up my brain.

The principal called my mother again. This time they decided that I would have to repeat the Spanish school year. But in order not to lose my Yiddish classmates they would let me go on into fourth grade with them.

The report cards were handed out at the end of the term. I knew what mine would be like but since Chabela was watching me, I smiled as if I had just been awarded a golden medal. I walked out of the classroom with my head held high.

The truth was revealed on the day the new period began. I was standing in line with the third graders, the only girl among twenty-four boys. Chabela saw me and gave Ana a nudge with her elbow. They both laughed.

School started on January 2nd. Although we were Jewish we celebrated *Los Santos Reyes,* the feast of All Saints, on the eve of the 5th. Following convention, I wrote a letter to the Wise Men. I asked them to bring me a bicycle with wide tires, but I didn't know if they would. When I woke up on the morning of the 6th, I got out of bed without making a sound and pushed the door open. There it was, a wonderful blue bike with thick tires!

I couldn't believe such happiness. I rode it for the first time that very day. My mother came out on the terrace with her American movie star magazines, and with one eye here, the other there, she kept watch over me.

"Don't you dare turn the corner. A madman could run you over," she warned me. There was also a family law that I must never disobey: I wasn't supposed to talk to strangers. This would spare me from anti-Semitism, envy, and, in short, all of mankind's evil.

But there was a problem. I liked Chava, my next-door neighbor, a blond boy with crinkled hair and a pointy nose. He was four years older than me. At night we would send each other messages in Morse code, using our telegraph kits. Chava used to play on the street with the rest of the children.

I knocked his ball with the front wheel of my new bike and turned to see if my mother was watching. Uf! luckily, she was intent on her reading. He smiled and said I should let them go on with the game. He thought my bicycle was swell!

"Till tonight," he said as I rode away. These few words made me happy.

A month after school began, a girl from another school came into our class. She had red hair and china-blue eyes. The teacher asked her what her name was. "Feigele," she answered in a small voice. He then asked what the meaning of the word was in Spanish. "Little bird," she answered again. With his hands he mimicked a bird's flight and we all laughed. "In Spanish it's Patti, isn't it?" She nodded and turned around to look at me. We smiled at each other.

Feigele was my first friend. With her I discovered the sweetness of having someone to talk to and to play with at recess. We competed to see who ran faster. The loser had to pay for our bag of potato chips.

When I was sure our friendship could be trusted, I told her I was going to show her something. I made her swear she wouldn't say anything. With one hand on the Bible, she solemnly swore she wouldn't tell anyone, not even her mother.

Chon the janitor was cleaning the girls' bathroom. I said I wanted him to meet my friend Patti. He looked her over carefully and trusting her fragile appearance, unbuttoned his pants and pulled out his huge purple thing. Patti screamed and bolted out of the bathroom. On the playground she burst out sobbing uncontrollably. "God will punish me," she kept repeating in despair. I tried to calm her down, assuring her God didn't exist.

For a week Patti behaved like a zombie. On Friday at recess she came over and said she wanted to see Chon's thing again. We shook hands and laughed delightedly.

114

After this demonstration of trust I asked my mother's permission to invite Patti over for lunch. My mother asked many questions about her. I didn't know how to answer, but in the end, she agreed.

It was the first time a friend came over to our house; that night I couldn't sleep. I was so proud that my friend was going to meet my parents and visit my house.

When we got in from school, we left our books in my room and went downstairs for lunch. Lucía brought deep-fried artichokes to the table. I finished eating mine and noticed that Patti was still chewing the leaf she had kept in her mouth; the rest of the vegetable was lying untouched on her plate. My father saw this too, and we both started laughing. My mother and Efraín laughed too. Patti didn't take her eyes off her plate.

Back in my bedroom she told me she was very annoyed. I tried to explain to her it was all a joke, but she wouldn't listen. I decided making friends was very difficult.

In the evening when she left, my mother came up to my room. She wanted to know what my friend and I had talked about. I told her I didn't remember. I had already decided never to tell her anything; I would keep things secret. "You must tell me everything, don't forget!" she said.

At the end of the term my brother was sent to military school in the United States so he would stop thinking of becoming a rabbi. His absence changed my life. I began to breathe more freely, as if a heavy weight had been lifted from my chest. Soon my dream of houses intensified. There was a wonderful world where everything was different from reality. People were always happy to see me there.

I learned to dream awake.

SWEET FIFTEEN

I was going to be fifteen at last. I had the feeling that my introduction to society would change my life completely. I would become a *señorita,* I would turn handsome like my mother, boys would start liking me, and everything from then on would fall into place.

My father had just bought a chain of supermarkets and was finally the man he had always dreamed of being; the same man who, one night, as a boy lying on the floor of a maid's room with three brothers and an empty stomach, had dreamed of becoming rich.

My birthday party was meant to be, among other things, a celebration of his financial achievement. For the memorable event, my father hired a huge ballroom and surrounded himself with the necessary people. He hired a troupe of decorators, stage directors and stagehands all the way from France. My mother, who was up to date on Hollywood's artifices, helped enhance the splendor of the party.

On a cold winter night, among a thousand astonished guests, I turned fifteen. To my good fortune I was known as being friendly and thus, I had fifteen dames and fifteen chamberlains dancing the Emperor's Waltz around me.

The day began with changes: they waxed my legs, they outlined my eyebrows; I was made up, combed and dressed. After all the effort, I still looked like a girl in disguise. Juanita, the hairdresser, assured me I looked very beautiful but the evidence was reflected in the mirror.

The climactic moment arrived. Trying to forget my excessive paleness and thinness, I listened to the twelve violins play a version of *Las Mañanitas* written especially for me. That was meant to be the first call for those of us backstage. I was to climb a ladder to the top of a basket suspended seven feet off the ground and filled with fresh flowers. Once I was inside, dry-ice smoke would be released and I would gently sway down amidst the clouds.

There was total silence. The chords of *Las Mañanitas* reverberated once more.

"Valeria querida, Valeria adorada, you were born on a cold winter morning…"

"Valeria querida, Valeria adorada, you are tender like a blooming flower…"

Oy vey is mir! My blue tulle dress that had been sent from Texas got stuck on a nail halfway up the ladder.

"Valeria querida, Valeria adorada, you smile like angels smile…"

"Go ahead, move!" commanded a voice with a French accent. "The violins…aren't you listening?"

I tried to unhook my nice dress from the wicked nail. The violins played for the third time.

Bathed in a cold sweat I pulled the dress. Cruaj! it ripped. I rushed to the top, climbed in and fixed the tilted crown on my head. As the basket was lowered through the now thinning dry-ice cloud, I started shaking. "You must smile," I recalled my mother saying. She's right, I thought. Otherwise they'll notice how ugly I am.

I stepped out of the basket, walked to the edge of the stage and descended the staircase, more with a grimace than with a smile. I marched across the red carpeted floor facing two thousand eyes. At the end of the aisle, a golden throne was waiting. My parents, one on either side, would make me queen for a night.

My conversion from child to woman was like a dream. My chamberlain approached the throne, and making a bow with one hand behind his back, told me I looked very nice. I danced with him as if it were all happening to someone else. In the middle of a cabriolet, he told me in a whisper that he had a present for me. He would give it to me in private.

After the banquet we went out into the garden. He gave me a little golden heart; he said I should open it. It had his photograph on one side, and on the other it said 'I love you.' Oh! he kissed me on the mouth and instantly we became sweethearts.

117

Our romance was short-lived because my father used to say Victor had a voice like Titino's, the comedian. And my father was always right.

MY FIRST LOVE

I buttoned my garter, slipped on my stockings and fixed my *postizos,* my falsies, in place. I drew the lines on my eyelids just like my mother did. I smudged pink lipstick on my lips.

My best friend Sandra had invited me to the party for her Sweet Fifteen's. The boys would arrive around four o'clock. There were five of us. *Pinguinas* was the name of our gang. There were five boys too, and they called themselves The Logic Gang. Oy! But it was Sunday and I had to eat lunch with the family and miss the luncheon and swimming in the pool.

By the time I got there, everyone was already in lively conversation. Sandra introduced me to her cousin Arturo. He smiled at me. I liked him immediately, but he didn't ask me to dance. Frida, on the contrary, knew just how to attract him. He asked her to dance and she never let him go. I noticed he was watching me. Susy—the oldest of the group—put on Elvis' latest record. I hated rock & roll; it wasn't romantic at all. Sandra didn't like it either, and since it was her party, she took it off and played "Love is a Many-Splendored Thing." I had recently seen the movie with my mother. Oh, how I longed to live a love like theirs!

Enrique and Susy were dancing cheek to cheek, *de cachetito.* I spent the evening with Memo, Samy and Lacho. They said I was very intelligent but I figured they liked me anyway. I didn't feel attracted to any of them.

When it began to get dark, the maids brought dinner from the kitchen. Arturo used this pause to tell me he had come to my Sweet Fifteen's *de gorrón,* without an invitation. I was about to ask who had brought him, when I heard a horn blow. "It's my parents," I cut him short. "But you just got here," he said. "I know, but I have to leave now." I waved goodbye to everyone and left the party.

The following day at school, I found out that Frida and Norma had both liked Arturo. They were jealous of each other and played out the competitive female scene. Afterwards, my very civilized friends decided that the one who was asked first would win him. I myself wasn't going to confess I liked him when he hadn't even invited me to dance.

A week went by without Arturo calling any of them. Then, one afternoon after class, as I was lying on the bed reading *Sinhué, the Egyptian,* Lucía came in to tell me someone was on the phone. "It's Arturo," she said. I rushed downstairs so fast I had to catch my breath. Don't get excited! I said to myself, he's probably just calling to get the number of one of your friends.

He had a low, sedate voice. He was calling to invite me to the theater and then out for dinner. I lowered my tone so he wouldn't hear my excitement and told him I would have to ask my parents. He said that he would call me back the next day. I hung up and dialed Sandra's number to tell her what had just happened.

My mother said that Arturo must come to the house first. He arrived in his mother's blue and white Pontiac. He was wearing a tie and jacket and had on *carey* glasses that made him look very masculine.

He inhaled my perfume when he greeted me and said he liked its scent. He asked its name so he could buy me the next bottle as a present. *"L'Air du Temps,"* I smiled.

My hands were sweating and my stomach rumbled. In the middle of these discomforts, Arturo said that people thought I was very conceited, *muy creída.*

"But I don't think they're right," he claimed with a smile. "Pretty girls always put on airs."

He was so handsome! I was sure we were born for each other.

He said he had better leave early so my parents would give us permission to go out together next week. We agreed on everything. As we said goodbye I noticed my mother was spying on us from her window.

When I walked upstairs to my room, she came out and asked me why such a young man wore glasses. "He looks old," she stated. Then she cautioned me never to let men touch me. "Otherwise they go and tell all their friends."

A week after our first meeting, Arturo took me out for dinner at the Czardas, a Hungarian restaurant where they played beautiful gypsy music. That night he gave me the newest version of "Autumn Leaves."

We made it our song. I used to play it day and night, thinking about him all the time.

About a month later, he invited me to dance at the Velvedere. At last my lifelong dream would come true. I would be going to the in-vogue place with someone I loved.

The nightclub was on the top floor of the Hilton Hotel. One could see the whole city from there.

I ordered a *medias de seda* and he asked for a gin fizz. We danced to the slow music. He was so tall I could lean on him and forget about the world. The orchestra played "Autumn Leaves" at his request. He put his big arms around my tiny waist and, whispering in my ear, asked me to be his sweetheart. I felt I was going to faint. But I said I would think about it.

The following Saturday, sitting in his car at a drive-in, I said yes. I didn't want to be seen there because my brother had recently told my mother he had seen Sandra and Enrique kissing at a drive-in. "Just like a tramp," he had said.

Later, when I returned home, my mother came into my bedroom. She said she wanted to talk to me; she asked me to make room on the bed and sat on its edge. Then she said that my father had made inquiries about Arturo's family and found that his mother had lovers. "And you know only whores do that," she added without a pause. "Your father doesn't want you to see Arturo again, or Susy and Sandra either."

I wanted to scream, "You can't do this to me!" but I knew there was no argument that would change her position. She hated Arturo and my friends, and my father hated whores.

"It's all for your own good," she claimed.

I lay in bed with my face buried in the pillows so my brother wouldn't hear me cry.

Our love story transcended the frontiers of *Pinguinas*. We became a modern version of Romeo and Juliet.

Arturo and I kept seeing each other secretly until he finished his training as a public accountant.

When he graduated, his parents threw a party in their garden. Arturo introduced me to his mother as his sweetheart. The woman smiled and said I was very pretty. She was incredibly handsome with red hair and shining gray eyes.

Arturo had a few drinks to gather courage and then asked me to be his wife. I held his arm and told him this meant a terrible problem. What would I tell my parents?

"We must face them," he responded. And I felt he was right. We cried and swore eternal love. Suddenly it occurred to us that if I got pregnant they would have to let us marry.

"Forget it, my father would kill me," I said, giving it a second thought. Arturo decided to speak to him. He was sure he would be able to convince him.

My father agreed to a meeting the following Sunday at our house. Arturo arrived exactly on time. He was nervous and didn't look too well. He told my father he wanted to marry me. "I can provide Valeria with everything she needs because I'm an accountant now and my father has just given me stocks in his business," he explained with pride.

Without any preliminary words to soften the blow, my father told him he could not marry me because his mother was a whore. I thought I would die when I heard him say this.

Arturo turned pale and jumped up from his chair, raising his fist. Suddenly, he stopped in midair.

"I'm not going to hit him because he's your father," he said, turning to me. Then he asked me if I would walk him to the door. Outside, he wanted me to tell him if I loved him more than anyone or anything in the world.

"We can run away and get married some place else," he said.

"I have to think about it," I answered, crying, and I kissed him goodbye.

Back in the house, my mother warned me that I would kill my father if I did anything foolish. She, who was well acquainted with sin, knew how to infuse fear. I felt I was going to die of grief.

Later that evening, an earthquake shook the city. *El Angel,* the statue of Independence, came crumbling down a few blocks from the Velvedere.

I knew it was a bad omen.

GRANDMOTHER GETS MARRIED

Since Grandmother had become a widow so young, she suffered greatly.

"It's no pleasure to be dependent on your daughters, I can tell you!" she used to say, her eyes filling with a dense liquid.

In the meantime her daughters took care of her.

Luckily, Grandmother had just discovered a future husband. He was a German Jew with a house in México City's wealthiest district, Las Lomas de Chapultepec, and a country house in Cuernavaca. Grandmother was not ambitious but she had been very poor as a child.

It all took place during an unpredictable fall when she, who had no friends, was invited by the Krausses for lunch at their home in Cuernavaca. Grandmother mused over the matter but finally accepted their invitation.

At tea-time, the German widower dropped by casually; the Krausses were acquaintances of his. The seventy-year-old man fell in love with Grandma on the spot. He seemed all right to her too. He wasn't that old and he looked clean, which was very important. She was excited; she imagined herself married to Hans. She wouldn't have to be dependent on her daughters anymore and she'd be as rich as they were.

Since she was a bit superstitious, she preferred not to speak about her love affair. Instead, she became the go-between for the Krausses' middle son and me. She said the young man was very interested in me, her single grandaughter.

Favor con favor se paga, one favor pays another. My prospective husband made a good impression on her.

"They're Lithuanians like we are, and you should see how devoted and respectful he is towards his parents," she said. "Besides money is not a problem for them," she added for my mother to hear, "they have plenty."

123

As I usually did on weekends, I spent the following Saturday at the Jewish Sports Center. The Lithuanian middle son approached me as if by chance. He was an insipid blond guy. Watching him, I realized how much my heart was still with Arturo. I hadn't stopped crying over him.

A few months after we met, in the same living room where my heart had been broken, Luis Krausse asked for my hand. I didn't want to live in my parents' house anymore. This time my father gave his approval immediately.

As all this was taking place the doorbell rang. My mother peeped discreetly through the curtains. "It's Grandma with her German friend," she said, startled. My father asked if she knew what was going on in the house. "She knows nothing," she replied warily.

Grandma came in, dressed in a strident tailored suit. As usual, she was wearing too much perfume; my father coughed. She grabbed the German's hand and, smiling with a hundred teeth, joyfully announced, "Dear children, I'm getting married."

And she married her third husband just a week before I married my first.

"Dear granddaughter, my wish for you is that you never need to depend on your children."

I on my part wished her great happiness and thought, *ay, Abuela,* with luck, this time it will last.

MY WEDDING

Luis and I had to get new passports the week before our wedding. I had to change my status in order to start my married life with my husband's last name. I almost cried when I signed in my new name.

As we were coming down the steps of the Foreign Affairs Building, I caught my future husband watching a woman's well-shaped ass. She was dressed in flashy red satin.

"Oh, you're vulgar!" I said.

"Why?" he asked, puzzled. I started a scene that surprised even myself; who would ever believe I was jealous? Luis kept swearing he hadn't even seen the woman. I said I was going to cancel the wedding.

"You can't cancel a wedding for a thousand people just like that."

"Oh yes, I can," I claimed.

The day of the wedding was cloudy. Early in the morning, the house was flooded with hairdressers, makeup stylists, seamstresses. It seemed like a repetition of my Sweet Fifteen. By ten in the evening, I had been turned into an astonishing woman. Just then, a storm began. My father called to say it was time to leave the house. We crossed rivers of mud and water to get to the wedding ballroom. It was twelve midnight. Greek statues surrounded the driveway; wet and naked they welcomed the guests. The bride arrived in a sumptuous car.

The chauffeur and the bodyguard rushed to help her. Pointing to the statues, the young bride told Juana, her maid, something that made them both laugh. *La niña* Valeria, as Juana called her, watched her father approaching hurriedly. His scar quivered on his cheek; his hat was big on him.

"Everybody is there," he mumbled nervously.

"I'm sorry, the weather is nasty," she said.

Her father adores her, the mother thought.

A sudden stomachache bent me over. "Ay!" was the first word I uttered as I reached the main door.

My father took me firmly by one arm; he was shaking. Mother took my other arm; she wasn't shaking a bit. I can still run away, I thought. The orchestra marked the beat: one, two, three, and played *Frenesí*.

"Walk and smile," my mother ordered.

The guests watched our entrance intently. The girl had already learned some important things concerning grace. As we walked down the aisle, we heard wings beating; hundreds of white doves were released from gold cages. Some of the men in tuxedos stood up on their chairs and were trying to catch the low-flying pigeons. My mother whispered that we shouldn't stop and, always smiling, we walked towards Luis, who was waiting for me. When he lifted the veil from my face a deep hush filled the synagogue. We stepped up to the *chupa* along with our parents. Four poles held the silken blue fabric woven with fresh white flowers. We took our places under the artificial sky. My jaw was quivering; I tried to compose an expression that would stop it.

The rabbi talked about our duties as exceptional sons and daughters of exceptional parents who belonged to the exceptional Jewish community of our exceptional México. I couldn't control my tears. The rabbi blessed us and placed the glass cup under Luis' shiny black shoe. He stepped on it, firmly, and split it in a thousand pieces. The rabbi blessed the cup. "So the Temple of Jerusalem shall never be destroyed again."

A peck on the lips, as bland as Luis' personality, sealed our union.

OUR HONEYMOON

Dawn rose over the Greek statues in the garden. A crowd had gathered outside the gate and was looking in, bewildered, while Luis waited impatiently for me to come down.

Hiding behind the curtains of her bedroom window, my mother watched me depart. I supposed she was crying because her little girl was leaving with a stranger she didn't love. I cried too without letting anybody see.

I stepped out the door, turned to look at the statues and said goodbye to Loba, my dear German shepherd who used to keep me company when I was sad.

We arrived in New York at noon. The manager of the Hotel St. Moritz welcomed us in; we were acquainted because I had stayed there with my parents several times. I was embarrassed that he knew this was my wedding night.

Luis and I decided to buy a couple of things in the drugstore around the corner before going up to the room. On one of the shelves, I noticed a little toothpaste and toothbrush kit that I thought could be useful for the trip. I handed it over to Luis to pay for it. He got red in the face and snapped that I didn't need that. The cashier turned to me, waiting to see what to do. I wanted the earth to swallow me up.

Out on the street, Luis asked if I was aware my father hadn't given him a dowry.

"Of course I'm aware. And that's why you won't buy me a dollar toothbrush?"

"A dollar is money," he declared. "Or don't you know that either?"

I noticed his ugliness, as if I were seeing him for the first time, and hated him with all my guts. I felt horrible when I thought I would be married to him for the rest of my life.

Back in the room, I went quietly into the bathroom, locked the door and sat on the toilet seat. I recalled a conversation with my friend Frida some months before. "You have to be careful," she had cautioned, "someone might want to marry you for your money."

"I'm quite sure that whoever does marry me will do it for love, not for money," I had replied, annoyed.

I heard Luis pacing up and down the room. Half an hour later, he knocked on the door and asked if there was anything wrong. "No, everything's okay, I'll be out in a minute."

I slipped into my transparent French negligee and put on the gold spike-heeled sandals my mother had bought for the occasion. I looked at my reflection in the mirror and thought, If only I could escape.

Luis stared when I walked into the bedroom. He walked slowly towards me and kissed me. I was repelled. I remembered my grandmother saying that a woman had to do her duty as a wife even if she didn't like her husband.

His tongue was like a mollusk in my mouth. He ordered me to bed in a whisper and without further preparation penetrated me.

The following morning we arrived at the docks to board the *Queen Mary* which would take us to Europe. A seven-day journey awaited us. As I stood on the prow watching Manhattan grow smaller and smaller, I listened to the languid song of the sirens and said goodbye to my dreams.

Our honeymoon lasted three months. Nine months later and forty pounds heavier, I gave birth to my first child, after a whole day of labor. He was a beautiful boy who weighed eight pounds.

Alberto became my only joy in life. His laughter, the first words he learned to speak, the first time he walked—everything delighted me immensely. My mother started calling him "her little Alberto," and treating him as if he were her own child. This troubled me but I didn't feel I had the right to say anything.

I used to put him in the bathtub at sundown with all the rubber toys Arturo had given me as presents while we dated. Alberto would push them underwater and watch them jump up, amidst peals of laughter.

When he turned ten months old, I made an appointment with the gynecologist.

128

"Yes, you're pregnant," Dr. Kuwatti said in his twangy voice. I was hoping he'd find another reason for my period's delay.

"A playmate is the best gift you can give Alberto," he added when he noticed I wasn't smiling.

I walked out of the doctor's office feeling giddy; I wanted to cry. It was so soon to have another child.

JUST MARRIED

Luis planned to teach me what a real woman was like. He wasn't a real man, I thought, so how could he teach me anything? The violence began.

The first thing he demanded was that I stay away from my parents. My household duties had to be performed to perfection: the meals, the clothes, the children. Since his own family was of utmost importance to him, my obligations towards them were endless. There were also the business engagements I had to attend to and, of course, I had to be a woman in bed. My life became a veritable hell.

When we used to fight, Luis always put forth his mother as an example. "But there's two generations' difference between your mother and me," I would complain.

His mother was the same age as my grandmother and was married to a very demanding husband. As *señor de su casa*, head of the family, he was due every attention, and even if he happened to be a tyrant—which he was—she performed her duties submissively...as all wives should. She was known for being a good wife and she took meticulous care of her reputation.

I, on the contrary, could never please Luis.

During my pregnancy, he felt he had the right to demand more of me.

It was a Sunday and we were invited to my cousin's wedding. I was surprised to hear my mother on the phone asking us to go with them.

Luis was in the shower and I couldn't say no. "We'll come pick you up," I decided. When he came out of the bathroom I told him that my mother had just called. "Well, if you said you would pick them up, you pick them up," he fumed.

I was furious; we hurled insults back and forth until we reached the point of hitting each other. He pushed me and I fell down on the floor. He's a scoundrel, I thought. How could he do this to me when I'm pregnant?

I went to lie in bed; I couldn't figure out what to do with my parents. I waited in the bedroom with the curtains drawn until it was time to pick them up, thinking Luis would feel guilty and ask for forgiveness. This he did, and a while later we were on our way. As we drove there, he threatened me by saying he would tell my parents. I begged him not to.

They had barely gotten into the car when he started telling them all about our fight, *con lujo de detalle.*

"She flung an ashtray at me. If she hadn't missed, I'm sure I would've been killed," he said.

"And why don't you tell them you had hit me and shoved me against the wall before I did that."

"You had insulted me!"

My mother and father didn't know what to say. One of them mumbled that we shouldn't be fighting while I was pregnant. To Luis that was unimportant; the essential thing was that I hadn't learned to be a woman.

I had a sudden headache and screamed at the top of my lungs. I asked him to drive to his parents' flat and tell them what he had just told mine. He asked me if I was crazy; didn't I know his father had a heart condition?

With the car in motion, I pushed the door open and felt an impulse to jump. My mother got ahold of my dress and my father, from the back seat, swung an arm around Luis' neck and told him to do as I said.

My in-laws heard the news impassively. His mother said we should solve our own problems. "How can anybody know who started the fight? She's no sweetbread, you know?" she added, nodding her head at me.

My mother was furious. "You know she's pregnant!"

My father-in-law took my father's arm; he said he wanted to talk to him in private and headed towards his bedroom. The rest of us stayed behind glaring at one another without uttering a word.

All of a sudden, we heard someone yelling for help. We rushed to the bedroom. My father was sitting on top of my father-in-law wringing his neck. Luis ran over and pulled my father from his.

"You know what he said to me?" he asked, addressing my mother. "That Luis is very angry with Valeria because we didn't give him a dowry."

"That's not possible," my mother kept repeating hysterically, holding her head between her hands.

I was crying in anguish. My father adjusted his jacket and told my mother and me that the three of us were leaving immediately.

How am I going to raise two children without a father? I worried as we came down in the elevator.

When we reached the ground floor, Luis was waiting on his knees in the lobby. He swore to me that he had a different viewpoint from his father's. He grabbed my dress and promised he would never, ever do a thing like this again.

I forgave him on the spot and told him he should hurry—we could still get to the wedding on time. The four of us climbed back into the car.

We entered the wedding party with smiles on our faces. We sat at a table full of people we didn't know. As I was tasting the soup, I felt my water burst.

After eighteen hours of labor I slept, exhausted.

"It's another boy," they told me when I woke up from the anesthesia.

Outside, it was daylight.

INTELLIGENT
AND HANDSOME

Those first years of marriage turned out to be so hurtful and discouraging that I was never able to fully overcome their effect on me. As time went by, Luis began to like and even love me, but I only felt like pushing him away. He was a premature ejaculator and I threatened to divorce him if he didn't go into psychoanalysis to solve his sexual problems.

Three months into treatment, Luis told me that Francisco, his doctor, wanted to talk to me. I thought I knew what was wrong with my husband but I hadn't dared to look into the causes of my own frigidity. I wasn't eager to see him, but I agreed to go.

I arrived at the doctor's office right on time; I knew he charged by the hour. When I had sat down, the first thing he asked me was if I had ever considered going into analysis myself. The question shocked me. I had always thought of myself as perfectly healthy.

After we had chatted for awhile, I confessed that I usually didn't sleep well at night. "That's why I started playing golf," I said. "Sports are the best cure for insomnia, don't you think?"

He suggested that I take a set of psychological tests. I wavered for a moment but then I figured that if it would convince him of my mental health I would do it.

The psychologist turned out to be a Jewish woman. My immediate reaction was to keep my mouth shut—otherwise half the people I knew would know all about my problems.

It was going smoothly until she showed me a series of black and white photographs and asked me to interpret them. In the first picture I saw a woman coming down a flight of stairs. Suddenly, ay! she tripped and fell.

"Go on," the psychologist urged.

I went running down the stairs to see what had happened. I couldn't believe my eyes. The woman, lying in a pool of blood, was my mother. I wiped away a tear.

"Go on," she pressed. With her cheap pen she was writing down every word I said in a little notebook.

Doctor Francisco called me the following week to tell me that he had read the results of my test. I went over to his office and before he had the chance to say anything I told him I wanted to go into analysis.

"Good for you," he cheered.

"And how did the tests turn out?" I asked.

"I'm not allowed to tell you. Revealing test results is forbidden in this business."

"After all the money and tears I've spent!"

He ignored my outburst and referred me to another doctor, someone he knew well. He assured me that he was an intelligent and extremely competent man.

"That's exactly the kind of man I need," I nodded.

My future analyst was short and bald. He hardly spoke a word; once in awhile he would ask a question. He was an orthodox Freudian and insisted that I needed to lie back on a couch for my ideas to flow freely into associations. He believed this was the best method for probing into the unconscious, "that river which governs our lives," as he called it.

Angry, I went back to Francisco and demanded, "How could you think that I would share my private life with a priest?" He told me to be patient, and I answered by threatening to leave therapy. He asked me why I wouldn't give myself the chance any intelligent person would.

"I don't understand what you're talking about," I said.

"Psychoanalysis is just for intelligent people," he replied, smiling.

And rich, I thought.

I decided to go back to my silent doctor but I had made up my mind not to say one bad word about my mother or father. I'm not going to fall prey to those clichés, I told myself, especially not with a stranger like him. The only thing left for me to do was to show him how intelligent and well read I was. I would talk unendingly about the books I had read.

Little by little, dreams started haunting me and soon my anxieties were surfacing. One day, as I lay on the couch, I was shocked to find myself crying as I had never done before in front of anyone. Where did all the pain come from? My masks began to crumble and I started feeling restless and fragile as crystal.

It was not long before I realized I had fallen madly in love with my analyst. Ay! It was the first time I had experienced lust for someone who would never feel anything like it for me. It was hell those three times a week I went to my appointments. I would walk in wearing a skimpy mini-skirt, lie down on the couch and tell him all about my unrelenting passion for him. Luckily he was ethical and resisted my advances unwaveringly.

A year into analysis I made up my mind to go to the University to study sociology. It felt wonderful studying again and for the first time in years my life had regained its meaning. My insomnia began to disappear slowly.

JUAN CARLOS

Marina was an Argentinian. Her father worked at UNESCO on a study project on Latin America's tropical diseases. Her life was totally different from mine. Her family had lived in various places around the world and that gave her a strange quality. Armando called her the Ethereal Marina.

Armando came from a working-class background; he was raised in *provincia,* not in the capital, and he had a bunch of brothers and sisters. He was a big affectionate bear, always a little in love with me—and perhaps I, a little with him too. Whenever he read St. John Perse, he shook like a leaf.

Hernán was Chilean. He had come to México right after the coup against Allende. He was handsome and had outstanding rhetorical skills, as most educated South Americans had. He said this was due to the fact that people were politicized in Chile. Whatever it was, he was much more outspoken than us Mexicans.

We were all students in the *Facultad de Ciencias Políticas,* the Political Science Department at the UNAM, México's Autonomous National University. The four of us were discussing the differences between Chile and México for a project in our course "Latin America's Sociological, Political and Economic Differences."

The doorbell rang. Without lifting her eyes from the paper she was typing, Marina shouted, "Who is it?" There was no answer. The doorbell rang again. She went to open the door and greeted someone with surprise. It was a man's voice; he said he was looking for her *compañero,* her boyfriend.

She invited him in and offered to make him a glass of *mate*—the Argentinian tea—while he waited.

"Te cebo un matecito," she said.

He walked into the room where we were working. He was tall and slender; he wore gray pants, a blue jacket, white shirt and a deep garnet tie. His elegance in this milieu startled me. He asked who I was.

"I'm Valeria."

"She's my classmate at the university," interrupted Marina.

He asked if his *mate* was ready. I said I would bring it in on my way out. He wanted to know where did I have to go. "Home to daddy and the kids?" he asked ironically.

"Right, on every count!" I said, smiling.

When I got up from my seat, he gave a short whistle, of the sort men use to flatter women in our Latin countries. *"Pero qué buena que está tu compañera.* What a good-looking broad, your classmate," he said, addressing Marina.

Hernán remarked he had to leave too; it was late and he must get back for Economics class. We all said goodbye. Armando announced he would be staying, although the presence of this *"patán creidito,* this pompous asshole," annoyed him, as he admitted the following day.

Marina told me that Juan Carlos had inquired at length about me after I left. "He was impressed, *che,"* she said, laughing.

Juan Carlos had been one of the leaders of Montoneros, the radical guerilla group in Argentina.

I asked why he had been dressed so elegantly. She said he was working as a high-ranking economist for the Mexican government. The man seemed incongruous. "That's life," remarked Ethereal Marina.

Juan Carlos arrived at five o'clock. He knew we were gathering again at Marina's. He came over, stared at me and, stroking his mustache, said, "I want to talk to you."

"Go ahead, by all means."

He demanded that we go outside.

"I can't," I said, smiling. "Today's the last day before we hand in our paper."

"I can finish it up by myself," Marina interrupted.

"Come on," Juan Carlos entreated, "I won't eat you."

"Are you sure? You look dangerous."

Marina came to the door to say goodbye. "She's one of ours," she told him with a smile.

"They all say that until the big moment comes, and then...."

Juan Carlos took me to his place, a tiny little house he shared with other people. I had the feeling I was doing something foolish that I would later regret. That's exactly what my mother would tell me, I thought and smiled.

"What's so funny?" he asked. "Are you laughing because I'm about to become your lover?"

"My lover? And how do you know you will?"

He pressed his body against mine and kissed my mouth to show his resolution. He was like a thirsty man just saved from a shipwreck. He placed his hands on my butt and squeezed my body against his.

I pulled my head back and saw black eyes that glittered like suns. He kissed me again, caressing my back, my butt, holding me tight. Just then, a woman who lived in the house walked across the patio. I was paralyzed.

He pulled me into his room. *"Sos linda y tímida,* you're beautiful and shy, right?"

The idea of someone having seen us together scared me.

"Oh, come on! None of these people are part of your world," he said, kissing me again.

This time, I put my arms around his shoulders. I liked this stranger but I felt compelled to tell him something before we made love.

"I'm not interested in your private life, *che.*" He forced me to silence.

Later, I was thankful for his self-possession, otherwise I would've regretted a confession that only sought to soothe my bad conscience.

We made love until there was not a minute left to snatch away. I had never known sexual pleasure, and now this Argentinian exile who worked for the Mexican government had come to show me what an orgasm was.

Juan Carlos and I saw each other every day for the next three months. During this period, Marina, Hernán and Armando—my three dear friends—included my name on the papers we were supposed to be doing together.

In the third month of our romance, Juan Carlos told me that his wife was coming back from Nicaragua. He had said he was married from the beginning, but since his wife had never shown up, I had conveniently forgotten. He wanted to keep me as his lover but I rejected the proposal right away. He said that I was like every other bourgeois woman; that I couldn't give up the

138

luxury and material wealth my despicable husband provided for a true love.

"You're just like every member of your class," he cried out in anger.

"And you're just like all the bourgeois men I know. You think you're so much better than everyone else, but I don't see any difference at all."

SANDRA AGAIN

It was a nice autumn afternoon. I was driving back from the university with only one wish on my mind—a bed to sleep in—when suddenly I saw a woman falling spectacularly down the front stairs of an expensive apartment building. I slammed on the brakes.

A man ran to help the woman but before he got there, she was already on her feet. Oh! it was Sandra, my old high school friend. I honked the horn but she didn't turn around. I honked again. This time she turned and recognized me. She climbed right into the car.

"Did you see how I nearly fell down?" she asked.

"Nearly?"

We laughed and hugged warmly. We began by counting the years we hadn't seen each other: five. Our husbands had disliked one another from the moment they were introduced and that had been the end of our long and warm friendship.

Sandra had become very attractive; she came from a line of red-haired, bright-eyed women. She said I was very thin but good-looking. She invited me over to her house so we could talk. I accepted, forgetting about my exhaustion.

I was in for a surprise: she was living two blocks away from my house. She had moved the month before. Our childhood dream of living near one another had come true. And me, what had I done with my life? I told her I was studying Sociology at the UNAM.

"Yes, of course, and I happen to be a cyclist, right?"

She wouldn't believe me until I showed her some of my class notes. But the best was still to come. Sandra had become a professional singer of Latin American music. Now it was my turn to be incredulous. My blonde and super-rich friend, whose husband was as jealous as a young Turk, was singing at a *peña!*

140

Impossible. When we got to her house, she handed me her previous LP of calypsos and sambas. After recording it, she had decided that, from then on, she would only sing the music of Violeta Parra, Viglieti and the other political folk singers.

"Our roads meet somewhere," I said. "Both of us have been looking for a way to go against the grain."

She inquired about Luis and my sons. She was surprised when I told her they were away in Europe for the holiday. "Without you? So, did you divorce?"

"No, we didn't get divorced, I just got liberated," I said.

That was a little too much for her to believe. She was suspicious to the point of calling Luis' office. When they told her he was out of town, she shrugged her shoulders and remarked, "Well, well, women's lib did you say?"

We spent hours in amiable conversation, drinking coffee and chain-smoking cigarettes. Late in the evening the phone rang and Sandra answered it. Immediately her voice changed: it became husky, deep. There were never-ending pauses. With eyes half-closed, she puffed out circles of smoke towards the ceiling. Now and then, she would laugh to affirm she was still there. She had forgotten all about me.

The black shadow of a tree could be seen through the window. *Hopscotch* lay open on one of the bedside tables. After the long languid whispering she said goodbye to someone named Margot.

"A woman?" I asked, wide-eyed. Sandra didn't know what to do with the evidence she had given me. I felt confused and excited. We sat on the bed exchanging nervous smiles, charged glances, moving silences... but unfortunately her husband Rafael came home. He was in a hurry, he was late for the children's baths. He hardly said hello. Sandra walked with me to the car. "He believes that if I bathe them myself they will fall off the bathinette," she said sarcastically. *"Házte fama y échate a dormir.* Build an image of yourself and you're hooked forever." We laughed. She made me promise I'd be back the next day.

I couldn't sleep wondering who Margot was. I set the alarm for five in the morning to finish a paper due at the university. Immediately after I'd delivered it I went back to Sandra's. She was waiting for me.

As hard as I tried to find out who the stranger was, she wouldn't tell me. First, she wanted to know a few things about me. Had I yet been unfaithful to Luis? Fortunately, there had been Juan Carlos with those wonderful eyes who, besides being a political exile, was a few years younger than myself. I stopped talking as I remembered how it all went wrong in the end. Sandra asked if I missed him. "Maybe," I said, "but I didn't want to become his official mistress, you understand?"

"And was he at least a good lover?" she asked.

"You haven't changed," I laughed. "And Margot, is she a good lover?" She blushed and gave a loud laugh. It was a delicate subject. Margot was the wife of her husband's best friend.

A few months earlier, Margot had begun making advances, but it was only recently that she had dared caress Sandra in the bathroom of the Muralto, where they were having dinner with their husbands.

As we talked, we drew near so no one would overhear us. "I liked it, why should I lie," she added, watching for my reaction.

The distance grew shorter. The following week, with a prolonged and electrifying kiss, Sandra and I became lovers. Uf! to discover I liked a woman! Never before had the possibility entered my mind. Christopher Columbus must have felt like I did when he discovered the Indies.

Luis came back from Europe with the children. Sandra invited me to join her acting classes; she said I had to meet Dimitrios. "You'll love him, he's got an incredible personality and his classes are wonderful." Sandra adored him and she soon coaxed me into seeing him.

It was true: he had a stunning personality and I immediately knew there was something I had to learn from this Greek.

But how was I to get Luis' permission to take acting classes? This was a problem. I tossed and turned in bed all night.

Part of my plot was to serve a perfect lunch. When we were through, we headed for the bedroom to rest as we always did. Surprised by my insinuations, he called the jewelry store to say he was not coming back to work. Now that he was no longer a premature ejaculator and I was no longer frigid, we could both make believe we liked each other. After the fiction was over, I let him know I would be taking acting classes the following week.

"Acting? What do you mean, acting?" He didn't understand a thing and I was compelled to use a few more sensual arguments.

Acting became my passion. "Getting to the climax of a scene is like having an orgasm," Dimitrios used to say. But some of my expressive capacities were blocked: hatred, fear, even love. On stage there was no way to lie. What a surprise for my ego! Dimitrios thought I should devote myself to becoming a director instead of an actress. But I preferred acting because I was really striving to become a writer. I wanted to live the lives of the characters, to move like them, to be them. And that I would learn only by understanding the workings of the stage.

A few months later, Luis and I bought a country house in San Miguel de Allende, just a block from Sandra's parents' home. Rafael and Luis at last became friends so they could play golf together.

On a Sunday, an unforgettable Sunday, Sandra came to visit me. Luis had just left the house. We hurried into the bathroom, burning with passion and expectation.

In the middle of a kiss and a *deshabillez-vous vite,* I glanced up and saw Luis in the mirror, standing at the door watching us. I screamed, pushed Sandra away from me, and went rushing after him. "God Almighty," he kept murmuring, rubbing his eyes.

Behind me, Sandra kept claiming it was the first time. She poked my ribs so I would back her up, but I couldn't; the evidence was all there. Feeling at a loss, she said she was leaving. She told me she would come back later and slammed the door on her way out.

Now that Luis and I were alone, he wanted to know all the details. After long nightmarish hours of questioning, I agreed to tell him a few things. What he most wanted to know was who played the part of the man, who the woman. "Of course Sandra is the man," he said with a guffaw.

His joke cast me into deep silence. Worn out, I lay down. He started pacing incessantly up and down the bedroom. At the break of dawn we heard a cock crow in the distance. I got out of bed and opened the window to get some air. I picked up the ashtrays and flushed scores of cigarette butts down the toilet. When I came back, Luis was already snoring.

The minute he woke up, he had solved the problem. Patting my head, he announced that what I had was an illness and illnesses can be cured. He was going to help me, he said, putting on his golf hat. He had an appointment with Rafael for a rematch; he had lost the day before.

Terrified, Sandra fled from my life. I only saw her now in our acting classes.

TO BELIEVE

"You have to believe in what you're doing!" yelled Dimitrios, beside himself. The student actors—as he called us—stepped down from the stage with heads down, unable to accomplish what he'd asked for. "If you're able to perform this exercise, you can consider yourselves actors," he had said. "It's a purification act and one that will require all of your skills."

He asks too much. It isn't easy to re-enact being born, I thought. I heard Dimitrios say it was my turn on stage. I was glued to my chair. He yelled, "Valeria, you're wasting our time!" There was no alternative but to face this final exam that would qualify or fail me as an actress. I lifted myself from the chair, feeling leadened, and walked towards the stage. The lights bathed my body; everything beyond the stage was dim. I couldn't breathe.

Breathe! I told myself. You're very nervous. But there was nothing I could do; air couldn't reach my lungs. I tried again, but nothing. Desperate, I fell on my knees. A violet membrane, like a mollusk, enveloped my body. I pulled my knees towards my breast and pushed against it. I couldn't tear it, not even a tiny hole. I tried once more. Gathering all my strength, I kicked again and again. I wanted to yell, "Don't let me die!" but I couldn't raise my voice. A beam of light crashed against the back of my eyeballs. A splitting cry ripped my throat. Dimitrios had turned the spotlight onto my face and was applauding, looking very moved. "You were born again," he said. I was crying desperately. He helped me to my feet. I caught a glimpse of Pepe wiping his nose with the sleeve of his overcoat.

The rest of the class was on its feet, clapping. Sandra was clapping too, but stopped when she noticed I had seen her. When I went back to my seat, Pepe told me he thought that my rebirth must have been a very painful experience. "Yes," I nodded quietly.

145

Sandra had promised her husband that she wouldn't talk to me again and she was keeping her word. I missed her a lot but I didn't want her to know it. Soon after the exam, Dimitrios got a job at the private TV network and abandoned his classes with no further explanation. Acting, and my love for Sandra, ended abruptly.

HEART FLIPS

Luis started treating me as if I were sick; it was the worst time in our marriage. Three months later, I was convinced I had to get a divorce, something which had been hovering in my mind since we first married.

We were separated on a weekend. It was hard to let the children know about our decision; they were twelve and thirteen then. It had taken me years to get to this point in my life and yet I didn't dare tell my parents. I let two weeks pass before I gathered enough strength to go talk to them.

My parents listened, stunned by the news. My father rose from his armchair and rushed towards me, shaking his fist. "How dare you make a decision like this without consulting me?" he yelled. I got up from my chair just as fast as he did and shouted, "Don't you dare, Father!" He stopped, sat back down and listened to me cry. After a while, he left the room; he had to go back to his office. As he reached the door he turned to look at me. I was unable to interpret what was in his eyes.

My parents had been aware that Luis and I didn't get along, but my divorce was a stain on the family's reputation.

The Sunday that followed our separation I was trying to figure out where to take the children without their dad. I was paralyzed and couldn't get out of bed.

Luis called around noon. He had moved into a shabby little hotel. Over the phone, he described his room without any wish to annoy me.

The one luxury item he had was a TV set on a mobile stand. While we talked, I listened to a voice off-screen. "I've lost my wife, children and home," he said, unexpectedly grief-stricken. "Wife and children! How is it possible?"

My heart was torn and I was crying for him. When he heard my grief he offered to come visit me. I agreed.

In front of the mirror I made my face up. Looking at my swollen eyes, my memory strayed back to the Sundays when my father used to take me for breakfast at Café Bolivar. Old refugees from the Spanish Civil War would say hello to him and smile at me. I was just a child, but he discussed business with me as if I understood every word. My poor father, I reflected. He never would have thought that a daughter of his would be a divorcée. I started crying again.

Just then, Luis arrived, unshaven and looking dirty. "I'll stay with you, if you want me to," he said. I readily agreed. "But you must go tell my parents and brother you're sorry. They're so hurt by what you've done to me."

"Sorry? Do I have to tell them I'm sorry for wanting to leave their precious little jewel?"

Steadying my voice, I told him he could leave now. He gazed at every corner of the room. I guessed he was thinking I was not worthy of it.

"You've ruined our lives already," he said dryly.

A damning fury took hold of me. "Leave and don't ever come back, you hear?"

"Are you sure? Won't you be crying later?"

I shoved him out of the room and locked myself in.

The following week I went to work in the sales department of my father's most manly business, the cement industry. I experienced the rigors of the man as well as his generosity. I had access to his fortune and the power this represented. But most important of all, I took back my maiden name.

MY MYSTICAL LOVER

For months I was haunted by the feeling that Luis would appear at any moment. But it was just an illusion. I asked myself if that was what I really wanted. Doubts troubled me. I wasn't able to enjoy my new life as a single woman.

My parents invited me to spend *Semana Santa*, Easter week, in Los Angeles. In the mornings, I used to stay by the hotel pool reading while they went out for a walk through Rodeo. One afternoon, while the sun was falling directly on my body, a drop of sweat slid down my naked belly. I wiped it off discreetly and opened my eyes. My brother was coming out of the gym, chatting animatedly with a very handsome man. He introduced him as Valentín, a well-known Argentinian painter who lived in the hotel. The painter scrutinized my body and, as if it evoked something, became thoughtful. He had strange yellow eyes. I remained lying on the chaise so the folds of my stomach wouldn't show, waiting for them to sit by my side. Valentín told us he had been living in the hotel ever since he had received "the call." I figured he meant the call of painting and told him I wanted to become a writer. Everything I had done in life, up until then, had been with the purpose of writing someday. Something seemed false in what I said. He asked what all those things were that I had done. I mentioned a long list of activities. No one was in a hurry to leave and soon the conversation turned into a tète-a-tète between Valentín and me.

Finally, my brother, annoyed at being left out, asked when Valentín could show us his paintings.

"Right now," he answered. I looked at my bikini. I had a long skirt to wear with it, but I said I wanted to change my clothes first. "You're fine just as you are," responded Valentín sincerely.

He lived in the Yves St. Laurent suite: a small, elegant, somewhat dark apartment. He said he didn't drink but if we liked, he would order something from the bar. I felt I should act the good girl and asked for a Seven-Up. Valentín said we were welcome to look but he didn't like to talk about his painting; he had a dealer to do that. So we didn't look around but talked about each other's divorces instead. My brother had gotten his a year ago, and I was only now beginning to enjoy mine. Valentín had been divorced for three years. He had two little girls who lived with their mother in Buenos Aires. As he talked, I glanced at a small photograph of Guru Maharaji under the desk's glass top. I asked Valentín if he was his disciple. "Do you know him?" He stared at me with wide eyes. I told him about Javier, a good friend of mine who had called me one night to say that a wonderful thing had happened to him. After many years of searching, he had found happiness at last. Valentín wanted to know more. I told him that Javier had taken me to the ashram where the Maharaji's followers gathered. On an altar filled with flowers was a huge photograph of a chubby Hindu in his twenties dressed in a white tuxedo. Javier had told me he was the Maharaji.

We had sat on the floor, listening to his adherents talk about their experiences with divine light, the nectar and the single sound. I'd felt a rush of laughter at the stiff way in which they told their stories. Javier and I had to leave the room. Valentín smiled; the anecdote didn't seem to bother him. He went on to tell us how he had met the Maharaji. He was still living in his native Buenos Aires, where he was a renowned heart surgeon. He had had everything he could wish for but was very unhappy. He decided to leave his work and family to follow the young master. Painting came to him like an illumination. Valentín had moved to Los Angeles to be able to visit the teacher in his Malibu home. His eyes shone as he spoke of the guru. I envied his inner peace and I promised myself I would look for the Maharaji after I returned to México.

When the Easter holiday was over, my family returned to México without me. Valentín had asked me to stay with him for a few days. I spent that first night at the Yves St. Laurent suite. As I was getting undressed, I saw his penis grow uncommonly large. He let out a Tarzan yell and his penis fell, head down, into his abundant pubic hair. He confessed that since his transformation he hadn't touched alcohol or women. I said he shouldn't worry.

He woke me up at midnight and, after a powerful and deeply mystical penetration, he began to cry like a little boy: he had lost his saintliness. Paradoxically, it was then that I realized I had to go back and find the spiritual peace I needed to write.

When I called him long distance a few days later, no one at the Beverly Wilshire knew where he was. He had vanished without a trace.

LOOKING FOR THE LIGHT

Guru Maharaji's ashram had re-located to Colonia Roma. Javier offered to come pick me up but I told him I would meet him there. He always wanted to end up in bed with me and I wasn't in the mood.

A high disciple of the Maharaji had come to México. I was lucky: he could give me the knowledge to gain the light. John was one of the handsomest men I had ever met. He lived with the Maharaji and the Maharaji's English wife.

In order to obtain the knowledge, I had to attend gatherings where people talked about their mystical experiences. I had to wash dishes, peel vegetables and polish floors as service to the Maharaji. The rigors of spiritual life separated me from the every-day world. I worried over what would become of me, but I was convinced I had to find something to keep me away from the problems of ordinary life.

Finally I was allowed to meet with John. There was a huge photograph of the Maharaji—this time dressed in Hindu clothes—hanging on the wall behind him. John asked me why I wanted to acquire the knowledge. I answered in the soft, slow tone they used, that the main reason was to achieve justice, social justice in this world. "And do you think you'll find the means to do that here?" he asked. "It's only here that I can find the instruments to accomplish this," I answered with humility.

The following day, John informed me that I wasn't prepared to receive the light. Oh, it was a blow. He must be a misogynist, I thought, and I hated his arrogance and his poise—his feeling that he was above everything that was human.

John would be leaving soon to go to the ashram in Tampico. Javier persuaded me to follow John until I was ready to receive the knowledge. I visualized myself as a disciple of Christ going after the Master. I boarded the plane that took me to the black-sanded port of Tampico.

John didn't seem surprised when he saw me.

The facilities at the ashram were minimal. I couldn't sleep or bathe there, so I took a room at the Hotel Camino Real. I used to get up at dawn and walk to the ashram, meditate, do service, meditate, do service and go back to the Camino Real. When contradictions soared and I grew anxious I would meditate again. After a few days, there wasn't a wrinkle on my face. I looked like a little girl again.

I had a week before I had to repeat the interview. On the consecration day, a gathering was held in a huge auditorium filled to the brim. You could feel the expectation among the silent crowd. I will have to leave my children, my parents, and I'll be forced into celibacy, I was thinking while they spoke. Suddenly I felt a rush of tears. People kept turning around to look at me. I couldn't stop weeping.

One of the brothers came over and asked me to go out with him into the garden. He talked to me about the congregation's joy at having an envoy of the Maharaji with them. He sweetly requested that I not disturb that joy and asked me to stay outside the auditorium.

This time, I didn't receive the knowledge either.

When I came back from Tampico I left the job as sales manager with my father's company and went back to the university to finish my Ph.D. in Political Science.

MUSICAL TRIP

Patti, my childhood friend, was very happy to have me back in the world of sinners. "I thought you were leaving with the monks," she said, smiling maliciously. I suggested we go to Europe together and celebrate. Her eyes shone but the glow lasted for only a minute. Her husband would never let her come with me. "Never say never," I said convincingly. Her husband, a good friend of mine, had recently confessed to me that he cheated on his wife on a regular basis. Patti didn't know, of course, and I was sure I could convince him with a friendly threat. "You're not such a son of a bitch to do as you please and have your wife live like a prisoner, are you?" I asked over the phone.

José agreed to let his wife travel with me, but he let her know that he was worried because I enjoyed too many liberties. *¡Ay, los hombres!*

After much thought, we decided to go to the Music Festival in Salzburg and then to Verona for the Italian Opera Festival. We sealed our agreement with a warm handshake. I felt like a teenager going on a summer trip with her best friend from high school.

I had a family affair to attend to in Israel, so I would meet Patti in Zurich, and from there we would drive to Austria.

I rented a car at the Zurich airport, a Fiat four-door with Italian plates. Fearful but happy, I cautiously descended the garage ramp and headed towards the Hotel Du Lac on the beautiful lakefront. Patti was waiting for me in our room with a bottle of delicious Beaujolais and gourmet hors d'oeuvres.

We left for Salzburg the following day. I picked the long road that crossed through the Shwartze Felder, the Black Forest. As soon as we entered, we were immediately immersed in the shadows of enormous trees, mainly conifers. It was a majestic forest stretching across deep mountains. I hadn't known that, once inside, we would constantly be crossing the border between Germany and Austria. We were asked to present our passports at every sentry box. Our thoughts began to wander over perilous ground—anti-Semitism, Nazism, crematories, dead sisters and brothers: an endless sequence of flashbacks. We were terrified. "It's very disturbing to see so many soldiers," Patti mumbled.

Night had fallen and we were still deep in the forest. We arrived at a small German village anxious to find shelter. The town's inn looked like a doll's house. It was clean as a mirror, though the bathroom was at the end of the corridor. As I fell asleep, I found myself dreaming of a room with an enormous fireplace. Men dressed with long white aprons were sliding stretchers loaded with bundles wrapped in sheets into the fireplace. The man in charge told me they were baking cakes. "You get out of here immediately, you hear?" he yelled.

I woke up screaming and remembered the bird children I had seen on the newsreel as a child. They had left their imprint on my soul forever.

Early the next morning we traveled through valleys of great beauty. The towns looked just like those from the children's story of Hansel and Gretel; old people still wore their traditional dress.

We got to Salzburg with renewed spirits. That very night we listened ecstatically to Beethoven's *Ninth Symphony* conducted by Von Karajan. With a lowered voice and with her eyes fixed on mine, Patti told me she was very happy. I felt a red cloud of desire come over my brain; I closed my eyes and squeezed her hand.

We went for dinner to a second-floor restaurant where we had the view of a charming fountain and we could watch the people passing by on the street. We were impressed by the Austrian elegance: men dressed in classic tuxedos and women in long black dresses were everywhere.

We left Salzburg on a rainy Sunday after a week of much music and contentment. Following Baedecker's advice, we took Freeway 5, but before long, we were stuck in the middle of a huge traffic jam. "It's getting late and we'll never be able to get out of here," Patti said with a worried look. "We should have known." Not far ahead, I caught a glimpse of a tiny gap where we could sneak in. *"Orale mi campeona!* Go ahead champ!" she shouted encouragingly, and to the sound of *"Viva México!"* I pushed the pedal to the floor and forced my way into the long line of cars.

The astonished driver behind us stepped out of his car, raging like a beast, and headed straight to our car. "Quick! lock your door," I screamed, rolling up my window. The bloodthirsty German raised his hand to break the windshield. "Please," I begged him, "don't break it, I swear I'll never do it again." It seemed written in the Book of Fate that the enraged man would change his mind. He glared at me and walked back to his car.

"Putane, ritornate a l'Italia," the other drivers yelled, when we had finally started forward again and they could see our Italian license plates. We were so relieved, we burst out laughing.

Verona welcomed us with its sweet Italian flavor. But three days of *Rigoletto, Aida* and some of Wagner's heavier pieces forced me to implore, "Please, no more music." Patti agreed, and so we spent the rest of our days walking across the cobblestoned medieval streets of Verona. Our spirits were well synchronized.

This childhood friend of mine, a Clairol redhead, caused a commotion among the Italian men. This helped to free her from fifteen years of bad marriage. But I kept telling her that to be able to talk of real freedom she should try to be more daring. Her aimless flirtation bothered me. As always, our differences in opinion made for fights. Our childhood conflicts returned as if by magic.

A week later, we took the plane back to Paris. Paris was like a second home to me. I was familiar with its nooks and crannies. I knew the most delicious cafés in which to spend an afternoon writing, drinking aperitifs and smoking Gitanes; I knew the small hidden churches where one could dream and meditate on every romantic possibility. But Patti wouldn't give me a chance to show her the Paris I knew.

THE MESSENGER

I spent my time in the Jeu de Pomme looking at the works of the Impressionist painters. On a sad afternoon, in front of a Manet sun dissolving into an orange sea, I noticed a woman who looked Mexican. She was wearing *huaraches Tarahumaras,* sandals made by the Tarahumara Indians, even though it was autumn—a Parisian autumn. I smiled at her and asked if she were from México.

"That's right, I'm a Mexican in exile," said the teenager.

At the Café La Fleur, she told me the long and sad story of her life. She had been born in Paris, but both of her parents had died in a car accident when she was very young. She had gone to live in México with her aunt and uncle who had a daughter just a couple of years older than she. Recently, things had grown tense with her adopted parents, and they had told Morena it was time for her to be responsible for her own acts. "So I came back to Paris," she smiled wearily.

I invited her for a pitcher of white wine in the bar facing the café. There, I talked with her about my mystical experience. I didn't have enough distance yet to draw conclusions. "But I have the feeling I was also running away from something," I said.

"Families don't accept the one who flees; it disrupts their order," she answered.

After the second drink, she said she had to leave in a hurry to feed Orlando. She asked if I wanted to come along.

She lived near La Gare San Lazare, and Orlando turned out to be a spectacular black cat that was about to deliver. Of course we talked about Virginia Woolf, discovering we both loved reading...and cats. No matter how dark her life seemed, it was easy to make her laugh. She lived with very little but she handed me a box of English biscuits, offering me some. Everything about her moved me deeply.

We arranged to meet on the following day at the Pompidou. There was a gigantic retrospective on Francis Bacon which we both enjoyed very much. She told me that her cousin back in México, Genovesa, was a painter. Their mutual grandfather was born in Genova and thus the name.

I invited Morena out for lunch so she could meet Patti, my lifelong friend. A few blocks from the hotel where we were staying was a small bistro famous for its soufflés: chocolate, cheese, raspberry...my mouth watered just thinking about them.

At the restaurant, there was a man who couldn't take his eyes off Patti. She kept smiling back at him, showing her willingness. The dandy turned out to be from Barcelona and invited her out for a walk and a drink of *calvados*. Patti asked me if it would be dangerous to leave with a stranger. "He looks like a nice guy," I said. I suggested she go ahead with "you know what...at least for once in your life."

"Nobody will ever know," added Morena, who was already acquainted with the subject. We arranged to meet Patti later at the hotel.

Morena and I went to Galeries Lafayette. I wanted to buy her a pair of winter boots. My young friend was moved to tears. "Please, don't mention it again," I said, feeling ashamed, and changed the subject.

She had the feeling that her cat was about to deliver that very day. I wanted to see how she gave birth so, after shopping, we took a taxi to her flat. Orlando had had the most beautiful little kitties I had seen in my life. I wanted to take one back with me. "Choose the one you like," she said. So I picked a black one with white chest and gloves on its front legs, knowing that I probably wouldn't be able to take it with me.

We had to hurry back to the hotel; Patti would be waiting. We were flying back to México at eight the next morning and we hadn't packed yet.

By twelve midnight Patti was nowhere to be found. "Why doesn't she pick up the phone, at least, to let us know she's alive?" I raged. At two in the morning, we started asking ourselves if the Catalán could have been dangerous. At four, I was ready to call the police. Our anxiety built by the minute until, finally, Patti appeared at the door. She wore a huge smile on her face. "Tell me something, did you at least go to bed with the Catalán?" I asked, dead tired and furious.

"No, we didn't fuck, if that's what you're interested in," she answered angrily. She only wanted us to know how she had debated between saying yes or keeping faithful to her unfaithful José. She uttered a romantic sigh and smiled. Her stupidity drove me mad.

Morena came along to De Gaulle Airport. When we were saying farewell, I told her that if she ever thought of coming back to México, she was invited to spend her vacations at my house. She thanked me and said she would come someday. "And please," she implored, "no goodbyes, they break my heart."

Patti fell asleep as soon as the Concorde pushed back from the gate. My stomach clung to my knees. The steward, a very handsome blond, came over after a little while and told me an engine was failing on this swiftest bird on earth. We would have to stay in Washington, D.C. and wait until the replacement part arrived from Paris. "In the meantime we could go to a disco," he smiled.

"*If* we get to Washington..." I added. Patti blew out a hoarse snore and woke up. When she noticed the attractive young man, she smiled coquettishly.

"The plane is going to crash," I said. She turned pale. "And you are going to get killed," she retorted. We didn't see each other for a long time after we got back to México.

III

FOREBODINGS

It was morning; reality had no shape yet. I drew my leg out of the sheets to feel the breeze on my skin. No one had made love to me in such a long time. That realization brought me fully awake. Suddenly I had the vivid image of Morena lying in a bathtub, dead. I jumped out of bed, picked up Genovesa's letters to read them over again and went out onto the terrace. I needed the sun's energy but outside I found a gloomy landscape.

The door of the aircraft closed with a muffled sound. I was left on the other side, missing and wanting you madly. The stewardess, a very nice French woman, said hello in perfect Spanish. I ordered red wine and toasted for us both. I couldn't stop recalling you; my skin was guilty for it. Dear Valeria, I have no idea what's waiting for me, but I definitely feel it's one of fate's calls, as you often say.

Genovesa had arrived in Paris and taken a minibus to get downtown where she had arranged to meet Morena. When she reached the station Morena wasn't there. Just as she was leaving, she saw Morena rushing in, dressed in black.

When she came in, she seemed to be walking in slow motion, like an animation fragmenting into colors. As we climbed into the bus that took us near her home, I finally looked at her. Her eyes were wide open yet she didn't seem to be awake. I asked her if she was feeling all right. There was something odd about her. I think I was afraid to admit it and I was lying to myself, thinking it could be something else.

Genovesa had spent the first few days without knowing what was wrong with her cousin. Later, she was forced to accept that there were signs of heroin use.

Morena told me she was going out with her boyfriend, a man who travels around the mountains of Europe collecting precious stones. He calls her whenever he's in Paris. I was very happy for her, poor girl; she spends so much time alone. She was supposed to be back at nightfall but it was very late and she hadn't arrived. Anxious, I called Luna, her psychoanalyst. She advised me to keep calm and wait. Her counsel was not much help; on the contrary, as time went by, I grew more and more worried. At sunrise, when I was about to call the police for help, I saw her getting out of a cab. She had nothing on except the white undershirt she slept in. I saw her open her handbag to pay the driver and then just sit there as if exhausted. She was drooling and her hair was disheveled. I got her out of the taxi as best I could and helped her up to the room. The next morning she confessed to me that she had managed to get the drug. She had injected it and had had a bad reaction. She was in a state of shock for many hours. Today she swore to me she won't do it again. Ay, Valeria, once again I'm losing hope. I don't know what I'll do next.

Following Luna's advice, they left the Arab quarters where Morena lived. This way, she would lose contact with the junkies who provided the drugs. They were living now in a proletarian district on the outskirts of Paris.

To escape the misery she was going through, Genovesa used to take the subway and get out at the Luxembourg to walk through the gardens. I was so burdened with images of death that I started thinking she wouldn't come back to me. It had been so long. . . .

THE ARRIVAL

Genovesa's fantasies recurred. She would be out for a walk around the Luxembourg Gardens when suddenly she would hear steps behind her. She would turn around. A long, gawky figure, dressed in a dark cape and wide-brimmed hat, would be walking nearby; it kept coming closer and closer. Frightened, she would walk faster; the figure in black would walk faster too. As she was about to run, the lanky figure would stop her. *It was you, my love. We almost made love in the middle of the park. I think only about you.*

Genovesa sent long, sad letters describing the ordeals she was going through. Morena kept promising her that she would get off drugs, but she simply couldn't keep her promises. It seemed she was unable to follow treatment for more than a few days in a row without somehow getting hooked again. Genovesa thought that only bringing her back to México could save her life.

Late one evening I received a long distance call. It was Genovesa. She was coming back to México with her cousin. She had threatened to leave Morena. "Valeria, I have nothing to do in Paris if I can't help her. Ay! love, if anything happened to Morena I would die of grief," she said over the phone. "There are moments when I act calmly, but sometimes I would like to beat her up to make her understand it's not fair what she's doing to her life," she added sadly. She was so relieved to have finally convinced Morena.

But there was something odd in the way she spoke. Her tone was cold, as if something had radically changed inside her. I didn't know how to interpret this. Suddenly, I feared the worst.

That night I had a dream. I saw them walking through a miserable neigborhood. Whores were standing in doorways selling their skins; junkies popped out at every turn, pushing death. Nothing seemed to touch Genovesa. She stopped to look at the facade of a deteriorated yet still elegant apartment building. Inside I saw a long dark corridor that opened to a brightly lit bathroom; Morena was lying in the tub, her face under water. She had drowned.

It seemed that from then on my mental clock was tuned to the cousins. I couldn't do a thing except think about them. How were they spending their last days in Paris? Morena packing away years of her life to return to México for good. She was one of those people who collect the strangest objects; her apartment in Paris was full of memories. And Genovesa? My heart leapt at the thought of her. What role was she playing now in her cousin's life, what were her thoughts...?

At last, the day of their arrival came. Early in the morning, I wandered out into the garden looking for flowers to bring them. I picked two roses: one blood red with a velvet texture and strong aroma; the other, pale white with a slight flush around its edges.

I wrapped them up in wet cotton so they would last until evening. Evening...how was I to muster patience? I wasn't good at waiting, so I decided to spend a very busy day. I picked up my manuscript and left the house.

The first step in the itinerary I prepared for myself was the Book Fair at Palacio de Minería.

The noon air was charged with dense grays and strokes of umber. My eyes hurt from the excess of ozone. There were hundreds of people inside the grand Colonial palace and thousands of books: books to buy, books to wish for; so many books you could vomit. Walking around in a sort of daze, my eyes were suddenly drawn to a purple hardcover. I noticed, with a sinking feeling, that it was the edition of Werther that Genovesa had sent me from France a few months before.

Unrequited loves; surely it is a bad omen, I thought. My blood rushed down to my feet. I elbowed my way through the crowd and ran in a panic until I reached the street. Once outside, I held the pages of my manuscript tight against my body and began to breathe freely again. They were my love story; the story I had been writing ever since Genovesa had left. Now, they only waited for her to read them. I began to feel myself again.

There were still a few hours ahead of me, so I decided to go into the Café Tacuba. I felt strong enough to bear the mistreatment of the ribboned waitresses who, since Don Porfirio's times, looked down on everyone who was not an aristocrat. I ordered a slice of sweet raisin bread and *café con leche*.

I took out my manuscript and jotted down a few corrections. The hours slipped by unnoticed and, before I knew it, I had just enough time to rush to the airport. Air France's huge aircraft was touching down as I arrived. Just then, a dense and muddy rainfall began. I hurried into the lounge to find a place in the first row of the waiting room. An ill-tempered woman who was standing at my side gave me a nudge with her elbow to force me out. "This is my place!" she yelled. I looked around and saw there was room enough for both of us, so I told her I was staying there. "Urban neurosis," I murmured, loud enough for her to hear. I shouldn't have said that; the woman started calling the security guard. Genovesa might appear at any moment and what would she think if she saw me in an argument with the police. Luckily, the guard seemed to think the whole matter was out of proportion, and asked the lady to move off a bit. Uf!

Meanwhile customs had filled up completely. Numerous silver carts darted along, piled with luggage; agents dressed in navy blue were checking every item. But my friends were nowhere to be seen. A group of men, part of a band, or maybe a soccer team, came strolling happily out, dressed in flowered shirts and pale-colored suits. The lounge was beginning to empty out. Suddenly I felt as if I had a hole in my stomach. Perhaps they had missed the plane; maybe they couldn't make it on time; maybe something terrible had happened. I felt a stab of pain simmering from the hole and I turned to find a seat.

When I was able to get up again and look, Genovesa was lifting a heavy suitcase off the moving belt. At her side, Morena looked like a zombie. I started waving my arms over my head. I wanted them to notice me, but they didn't even turn around. I tried again but this time I only managed to knock my wide-brimmed hat. I had dressed exactly like Genovesa had described the character in her fantasy, and she didn't even look up once!

Finally they came through the revolving door. Morena looked like a dead person. She was carrying a small wooden box tied with coarse string. Her face was ghastly, covered with acne. When Genovesa saw me, she lowered her heavy suitcase to the floor and walked over. She was as cold as the Antarctic. She gave me a kiss on one cheek, a kiss on the other, and then she let her eyes wander to see if anyone was watching. Feigning calm, I gave them their flowers—the white one for Morena; to Genovesa, the red one. "Accurate as always" was Morena's remark.

My black Mustang—so important to this story—was now covered in a mud-splotched cloak. This was México City's harsh welcome and I suddenly felt sorry for us. They were both quiet, as if there was nothing else to be said; as if everything, after all, was there to be seen, everything was evident. I was feeling nervous and kept asking questions about the trip, about their last days in Europe. I talked about the arrangements I had made to welcome them home.

Morena interrupted me by handing me a cassette to put in the tape deck. The music was too loud and I lowered the volume. "Turn it up," she snapped dryly, "so we can hear it." Genovesa was staring straight ahead and her eyes didn't blink. I don't like this, I thought. Obviously there's something wrong.

Meanwhile, the city's public transit signs kept directing us along detours, exactly as it had happened months before when Genovesa had left. She seemed totally unaware.

Evening descended on us like a plague. We stopped at a traffic light. A yellow and violet neon sign striped our faces. Genovesa put her flower on the dash. The silence, the abandoned rose, the scattered words....A frosty breeze slipped through a crack in the window.

Morena said she'd rather stay at Genovesa's studio and get some rest. I could see she was completely exhausted. Genovesa was exhausted too, overcome by death, worried for her cousin. "I can't leave her alone, she's too sick," she grimaced.

All my plans fell apart.

DESPAIR

The monkey licks my monkey. Alameda kisses my snout with canine laps. The anise falls on the bed. I smoke a joint of golden guru and ascend to the place where colors are luxuriant. Leggy little animals hang from the curtains; they stick on the mirror. I masturbate: ayyyyy! I hear a scream, my breathing is paralyzed. Penalty! A gunshot closes the race. Handke's porter holds his head. The zoo comes back into focus: one little monkey, two little monkeys, really dirty, come out from under the desk. Aj! how disgusting, I had forgotten all about them. I must get rid of them.

It's not fair, always waiting for the phone to ring...waiting to hear from her, who now only cares for the sick. I hate Morena, she's taking my lover away from me. Damn it! I've never hated so much. My fury grows, it goes up and down my veins and arteries, it petrifies. I must kill her, oh God, I need to reach Nirvana, an interior light that depends on nothing outside.

Utamputa! the hello, hello artifact is ringing.

"Morena, is that you? You want to know why I'm mad?"

The scene seems a repetition of another scene.

"You ask why am I *tan naca?* Do you know why Cortázar said *ata la rata* and Goya said the *Maja es Maya.* Do you know why?"

While Morena covers her mouth to keep from laughing out loud, I listen to the stampede of a dying blues. Armstrong smooths his lips and vocalizes, "I'm with you baby."

"I don't want to see you again, you hear?" I hang up the phone. "Aba Ima, Pater Nostrum: forgive me for everything."

Another drag and I see Kandinsky lines. A woman appears to have found her exact form: a bird woman, a triangle woman— an elbow, a breast, the nose of a bird. The woman turns to the camera an eye of madness. An old sadness is captured. Click.

169

When the midnight bells toll, Genovesa walks in and lets her brown overnight bag drop at the side of the bed.

"I hate words because they try to pin everything down," she says.

She undresses without preamble and kisses me.

"Love, what's wrong? You look terrible," she says, distressed.

"How sad. Such craziness...I should..."

"Hush, you should nothing." She pushes away the monkey's bottle. *"Anís del Mono.* Is that what you're drinking?" she asks. "Oh god, you're weird."

She glues her body to mine. The instrument that freezes moments clicks. I cry and kick, immersed in the sea of my fantasies.

A VIOLET DANCE

Images of water and wind. Three people stare into space. They are sitting on a faded green sofa. Janosh, with his unbearably crooked nose, straightens up; Morena, off of drugs, perches on the arm of the sofa and holds on to him. Genovesa walks up to the record player and turns the volume up. Patti Smith sings "Horses." Genovesa squats and follows the rhythm. Her dark skirt with yellow flowers flows against her hips.

Johnny takes out a sharp pocket knife; with one movement, he slits his jugular. He falls slowly on the wet sands of the beach. A throng of horses moves towards him; deep red tongues of fire rise from their velvety snouts.

> There is a little place called space.
> The waves were coming in like radiant stallions.
> There's a little place called space.
> A promised land.

Genovesa pulls herself up, arms akimbo, and takes her place next to Janosh. The thread of this story is accompanied by the dry hammering of metallic brushes. The three characters facing me look like the portrait of a deadly rock group. Time drifts by without clearing the pools of darkness in my mind. I suffer from the past weeks of infrequent amatory encounters with Genovesa.

A woman dressed in white walks towards Johnny; she picks up a box of white powder, decorated with violet flowers. Johnny inhales; they kiss. Johnny and the woman make love. A thread of blood runs from Johnny's mouth.

Genovesa slips her tongue into my mouth; she runs her fingers along my body.

> There is a little place called space.
> There is a promised land.

She puts my hand on her belly. A ray of light breaks the studio's perfect curve. She and I become two perpendicular lines; we dance on the bright wooden floor. As evening sets in, our mood declines. The mirrors cast images back and forth.

The waves are coming in like radiant stallions.

Johnny's life is lost in a tide of the night. The paw, paw, paw of cymbals flash tiny circumferences all around me....

Suddenly Johnny gets the feeling he is surrounded by
horses, horses, horses coming from all directions
White shining studs with their noses in flames.

Johnny sees horses, horses, horses, and sings, slipping away; he knows how to flow. And goodbye boys, look at the crocodile in the flux, see how he makes love to his sister and see and see how she moves her hips; and look, look at the horses galloping on a rising sea; and see how she moves her hips to the rhythm of Horses: the metallic brushes pam, pam, pam; Smith's voice; the guitar; Genovesa's skirt moving against her hips, flows, flows and I want the woman. My gaze locks hers, she knows what I want...and moves and moves her hips, she moves them for me and I want her, and desire becomes furious. Janosh dances with us; dances and accompanies our desire. Morena holds him by the hand; they both dance to the paw paw's rhythm. They disappear as if by magic; they enter the empty room and fill it with their presence. They plot long-winding roads....We lock ourselves in Genovesa's room.

The bed is covered. We are both dressed. We kiss. She takes off her clothes, my clothes, we take off our clothes together to the rhythm of the watusi. The rhythm becomes swifter. The world disappears, infinite tides, deep waters, luminous blacks. The earth covers with moss, her vagina awaits me, my mouth, my tongue, her clitoris, her pubic hair, our smells and tastes: two invaded territories. A parenthesis in space: time quiets down. She and I: memories rush in, I hold her, she holds me, they come and disappear. We are sitting: our vulvas touch, each feels the warmth and humidity of the other. Mmmm, we kiss, caress our backs, we laugh and purr like happy cats. "Put on music that makes me feel fearless strengths, hands, tactile tongues swift as the flames that lick the logs," I say out loud. The bed is ready in a second. The dice are thrown. We make love as if there were no yesterday and no tomorrow, our whole attention concentrated on the present.

The next morning when we woke up, Genovesa left a note for the others: 'I'm going to Valeria's house.'

"Life has its do-re-mi flats," she said, feeling threads and ropes loosen. She had finally freed herself from what had tied her to her cousin. My house was filled with *Siglos,* luscious food and joy. We loved each other again and, once more, fear vanished. We began a new cycle.

AGUSTÍN

Agustín, my right hand man, was sick. The doctors repeatedly claimed there was nothing wrong, but the pains in his lower stomach would bend him down and leave him gaunt; he lost fifteen pounds in one month. "In Guerrero, there's a *brujo*, a medicine man who cures everything," his brother told him. I pictured Agustín under a blue sky, climbing up the steep trail on his horse. There was the smell of fields and a pressing heat. Old brujo Bulkabú, king of the monkeys, dressed in palm cloth and blue rubber sandals, was sitting on a little wooden stool waiting for the sun to set. His skin was black and sweaty and his tits hung. He had gray beehive hair. Next to him, a gaunt woman was chewing on a red fruit; her teeth had picked up the same red colors. She was molding a clay pot and had eyes that stared into emptiness. Famished dogs wandered around their ill-starred young.

Agustín was ordered to lie down on the worn-out mat covering the mud floor. Lying like a dead man, he noticed the offering of weed plants and amaranths on the dark Virgin's altar. Without stirring, the brujo took a sip of alcohol and spit it, fan-like, over the possessed man. The wind urged a rush of dirt. Bulkabú, king of the monkeys, drank again, and again spread out a shower. The toothless woman laughed with a hoarse voice as she fanned dandelion herbs over the sick man. Agustín was urged to change his name to Salvador Diente de Oro. When the name Salvador Golden Tooth was said out loud a spark flashed across the shack. Bulkabú ran his hot sweaty hand over Salvador Golden Tooth's limbs: flash.

Gathering concentration and sweat upon his chin, the brujo opened his closed fist, made a jigsaw with his right hand, placed it over the skinny victim's swollen belly and, to the rhythm of *duro y dale*, cut the stomach which didn't bleed but stayed imaginarily

174

open. With a firm hand, he extracted a tumor covered with hairs from the contrite belly and submitted it to the fire. After the miracle was performed, Salvador Diente de Oro sang praise to the Virgin Mother of the Mexican people. Bathed with the healthy sweat of the cure, he was invited to share a drink of alcohol. Bulkabú saw how he brought the anise to his lips and heavily tipped the monkey's bottle. Everyone laughed. Two months later, Agustín died in the Clínica Londres.

My fate—my legacy as a woman—worsened with the loss of this faithful man. Lola, Mercedes and María, when confronted with the transcendental event, left without saying goodbye. The work of supporting eight hundred square meters of property was left in my charge. With the strength of a goddess, I refused to be walked on by my sons. Serious problems arose: the boys claimed they weren't meant for domestic labor. This claim symbolically closed the circle my father had spun around me when I was born. The price of freedom would be a heartrending break. Agustín's death had been the detonator that brought this dark truth to the surface.

ONCE AGAIN?

In the midst of these changes, I decided not to lose the tan that was essential to keep face, so I went onto the terrace for a sunbath. I was having difficulty concentrating on my diary when the intercom buzzed. Alberto told me my father was on the phone. My heart leapt. My father's voice was dry; he said my mother had one of her customary migraines but this time it was worse. I had to go see her immediately.

I threw on a shirt and jeans over my bikini and ran to their house. Her bedroom door, usually locked, was ajar. The curtains were drawn; inside, everything was dark. "Who is it?" she asked, frightened, when she heard me enter. "Valeria," I answered. Headache and all, she managed to ask sarcastically how it was I'd had time to visit her. Ay! my mother, she doesn't change, I moaned in silence.

I pulled the curtains open and noticed there was a camphor-smelling rag covering her forehead. I asked if she wanted me to call the doctor. She nodded and lifted the rag off her head. The muscles in her face were contracted; she looked a hundred years old. I felt deeply sorry for her. When I got him on the phone Doctor Brussy assured me he wouldn't be long.

I placed my hands on my mother's forehead. I had never in my life touched her before. It made me dizzy. I forced myself to keep my hands on her face and massaged thoroughly the tension knots that had formed on her neck and face.

I noticed there were tears sliding down her cheeks. I cried quietly with my poor mother without letting her know it.

"You have a saint's hands," she said, opening her eyes. Just then, two male voices approached the door. They were my father's and my son Alberto's. My father asked, "How is she?" motioning with his head towards my mother. She herself answered that she was much better because of the massage I had given her. My brother came in from parking the car in the garage. The scene surprised him. I took my hands off my mother's head immediately. His interrogation began: what medicines, how many, at what time? She answered each of his questions wearily.

I decided to leave the room so I wouldn't have to hear. My father and son followed behind. We sat in the antechamber: we had nothing to say to each other. My father picked up the first section of *Excélsior* and started to read. I leafed through the pages of the last issue of *Hola*, the Spanish magazine, and read the gossip that Julio Iglesias' wife, a gypsy beauty, had married again, this time an Arab millionaire. My son was studiously going through a computer magazine. Just then, the doctor arrived. He kissed my cheek and shook hands with the men. He asked to be left alone with the *enfermita*, the little sick one.

My son had to run off for lunch; he had an appointment in his office at four o'clock. Now that he worked with my father, he had become quite the businessman.

He asked if lunch was ready at home. His question puzzled me. I said there was always lunch in the house. I saw he was up to something; he obviously wanted my father and brother to know how wrong things were since Agustín's death, how I wasn't performing my duties. I won't fall into the trap, I told myself. "We only miss lunch when there's no cook in the house," I answered.

"In our house," remarked my brother in his pompous tone, "lunch is always ready, and you can come whenever you like. Ay, the poor boys, they're worth gold," he added with a moan.

"And who do you think gave birth to those...golden boys?" I asked. As if he hadn't heard my question, he went on to say that they didn't deserve a mother like me. "And you," I said, "you have no right to intrude in my life, you hear?"

"You're a bitch, that's what you are!" he yelled.

I wanted to appease him but, as usual, I did the opposite.

"Y tú un pendejo, and you're an asshole." I knew immediately I shouldn't have said that. My brother rose from his chair and approached me with stiff knees. Giving me no time to react, he slammed my face with his hand. This time I won't let him, I thought. I stood up and punched his face with my closed hand; I felt his eyebrow under my fist. He had studied karate for years and he responded with a series of kicks. I swiftly avoided them,

177

making him lose his balance. Feeling a newborn courage, I struck him again on the same spot.

His eyebrow began to bleed. He touched the wound and looked at his fingers. He grabbed me by the hair and pulled me out of the antechamber. My father was trying to scream "Let her go!" but his voice was too weak.

We reached the inner garden. There, he forced me to my knees and struck my head against the tile. The courage to defend myself vanished once more, like it always did, as he kept on beating me. "Help!" I yelled desperately.

My mother and Dr. Brussy came out to see what was going on. "He'll kill her!" my mother screamed.

Brussy got a hold of Efraín, took him by the elbow and told him in a quiet voice that my mother needed rest. "Go home and come back later," he added, taking him to the door. My brother obeyed but didn't stop shouting. He yelled again that I was a bitch and that I didn't deserve the children I had.

I got up from the floor and went to look at myself in the mirror. I had a fleeting eye like Sartre's. Brussy diagnosed a splintered skull. My mother's headache had disappeared.

SCARRED FACE

A man with a face scarred by time guides me to a room. Inside, everything is extremely blue and plastic-like. I'm intimidated by the many doors. Where do they lead? I ask myself. Time expands, I stay awake all night. The morning light enters through the window like an awaited sign. I dress up quickly. According to previous instructions, I don't eat or drink anything. I try to remember where I saw the elevators last night. I push the button that says SW. The metallic box descends several floors below ground level. Long rubber lengths muffle the steps of passersby; everybody seems to be sleepwalking. At a distance, I see arrows indicating the direction I must follow. Data accumulate, giving me a hard time. "Step by step," I say to myself. I walk into an elevator of even numbers. The ascent is dizzying. When the doors slide open, I turn right. At the reception desk, nurses—young and old, all dressed in white nylon, all of them sexless—are working away. I approach the one who looks most friendly. She hands me an envelope and smiles. The lounge, at my back, is filled with mustard-colored sofas where old, very old people sit. A woman stands up; I sit in her place. I take out the perforated cards from the envelope. Step by step, I repeat to myself. I hear my name called through the loudspeaker. I flounder. The nurse has forgotten to give me the most important card.

"When you are through with your exams, go over to Doctor Helmut Gantz's office."

I return to the long silenced corridors. At every hallway turn, there's a round-faced clock. I come and go, climb up and down: I have to keep on walking with unchanging pace. I'm thankful that Genovesa packed my walking shoes in the suitcase. I pick a card from the envelope that looks different from the rest: Lunch Time. A sign that reads Quick Service appears before me in one of the corridors. A waitress suggests the full meal; she orders it through

179

a walkie-talkie. At a distance, the man with the scarred face is setting napkins on brown trays. I pay the cashier.

I walk towards Dr. Gantz's office. He observes me through rat-like eyes. He makes a point to say that the most important test is yet to come: the lung examination. He rings a bell under his desk. A handsome nurse appears holding a robe and blue slippers. She puts them on my feet, sits me in a wheelchair and calls on a muscular young man who pushes me to a door that reads Special Care.

A doctor with a surgeon's cap on his head comes out to get me. Inside, everything is covered in white tiles and smells of medicine. He informs me I will be put under anesthesia for the exam. "It's a serious test," he warns. Strapping my arm with a rubber band, he pinches my hand. I hear a huge machine approaching on rubber wheels. They're going to thrust a tube down my throat but I'm not sleepy yet. I want to scream, I want to tell them not to do it....

"Why are you screaming, love? What frightened you? Wake up. You're here with me, calm down."

"Oh, it's so good to have you," I said, sighing with relief.

THE APPOINTMENT

At eight on the dot I was standing at the door of the restaurant where my father had arranged to meet me for breakfast. A liveried valet took away my car. I had gone to bed late and there were black rings under my eyes. As someone opened the door behind me, a wind came rushing in and removed the scent of my perfume.

My father avoided the kiss I gave him. The maitre d' led us to a table overlooking the well-groomed garden. He left the breakfast menus on the table. The guests were mainly men; they looked exultant, without worries. My father confessed, with a hint of revulsion on his face, that lately he didn't enjoy food. "What a pity," I said, looking out the window at a hummingbird balancing itself on top of a sulphur-colored snapdragon. I was certain I had inherited my love for life from this man. I repeated that it was a pity. My father waited for coffee to be served before he listed his worries. "Your sons will soon be married and you yourself are not getting any younger, you know?" He wanted to be explicit about my need to remarry.

"I'm not thinking of getting married again," I interrupted. "The only thing that interests me now is writing."

He gulped his water down and coughed. He answered, practical-minded as he was, that there was time to do everything. I wanted to tell him that women in my social position were allowed to do anything as long as we didn't take it seriously. But I kept quiet. My silence irritated him.

"You think you know everything, don't you? But you're wrong."

I was afraid to fuel his anger so I said nothing. When he saw I wouldn't give in, he played his last card.

"I've been thinking of having you and your brother inherit while I'm still alive." He asked for the check. As the waiter was serving more coffee, he added, "An apartment in the United States or Europe and money to keep it."

A place that I could share with Genovesa, far away from México: the thought of it made me feel faint. His offer could mean my freedom....The illusion lasted only a minute. His gift would be subject, precisely, to my leaving her. Furthermore, we both knew I would have to wait for my oldest son to marry, then for the younger one to do so too. Later, they would both have children and I would have to wait for that also. And then, who could tell, maybe then I would be free. But who could really tell?

My father looked at his watch: he was already late. The liveried valet brought his car to the door. I saw him leave in his gray limousine, driven by the chauffeur who had worked for him for years. As they sped away, I had the prescience of something cold and hard coming between my father and me. I felt the swell of tears in my eyes.

In the evening, Genovesa and I went to see *The Bitter Tears of Petra Von Kant* for the third time.

"Do you think your father knows about us?" she asked.

"Yes, but not consciously," I said. "He prefers it that way."

Someone in the back told us to be quiet. "Why don't we leave," she suggested. "I feel like making love."

"You always feel like making love."

"Yes, that's true, and what about you?"

"I do too."

At sunrise, Genovesa woke up screaming. A cat had slipped in through the bedroom window and was eating away her clitoris....

"Ay, how awful! But it was I who should have had that nightmare, not you" I said.

She hugged me, kissed me, licked me. "I'm glad it was just a bad dream," she said.

MY FATHER'S LEGACY

The months that followed were violent. Genovesa's small car suffered damage. One morning we found its windshield shattered to pieces. A week later, the driver's door had sprouted a large dent. Even though I refused to acknowledge it, I had the feeling my sons were to blame. In the end, I had to accept the sad fact. Genovesa suggested I talk to them.

"And what should I tell them? That I love a woman?"

She insisted that it was much worse to leave things as they were. "Up until when do you plan to keep hiding yourself?"

My worries as to how to tell them made me lose sleep. In the end, I decided that talking to them would be like proclaiming my own death sentence. My conclusions were definitely drawn from fear and I knew it. I was afraid my sons would never forgive me; I was afraid my father would consider me dead. Impotence stifled me.

At home, the atmosphere threatened to bring out the beast in all of us. The idyll I had lived with my children was about to end abruptly due to forbidden loves and economic interests. We were quarreling about everyday matters: the food, the clothes and especially mother's friends.

The lucidity I had found during the breakfast engagement with my father began to wither. I decided to pay him a visit at his office and find out if the gift he had promised was still offered.

The first thing he said when he received me was that he was fed up with life. His success hadn't brought him the happiness he had expected.

He had recently come back from New York with my mother. He described to me, with an abundance of details, the apartment he had found for me: an extraordinary high-rise, a hundred stories tall overlooking Central Park. "Sealed, so you can't hear the sound of the ultrasonic Concorde."

A spectacular showcase for millionaires, I thought, picturing myself alone in a cold, empty place. The image was pathetic.

"I'd rather have a flat in San Francisco," I said. "New York scares me, all those inhuman high-rises."

My answer surprised him; he lowered his gaze and, for a moment, doubted whether he could make me yield. Finally, he said I could go look for an apartment in San Francisco with my mother.

"With my mother!" It was my turn to be surprised. Why is it always like this with my father? I thought as I walked out the door. I can never get what I really want.

JOSEPHINE'S BATHS

On a rainy May morning, Genovesa and I boarded the plane to San Francisco. We arrived in time to admire the sea surrounding the harsh hills of the peninsula.

I had reserved a room in a former boarding school for young ladies that had been turned into a hotel. The idea seemed very exciting.

Genovesa was startled when the taxi stopped in front of a hill of well-groomed gardens. The old house stood on the summit. We climbed through hedges of hydrangea and patches of perfectly manicured English grass.

A woman dressed in the English fashion of the nineteenth century, wearing a white coif and long apron, came to greet us. The taxi driver—a pure-bred Italian—walked into this atmosphere of dark woods carrying our luggage. "Wow! This is something special!" he gasped.

A man with a baritone voice told us there was a little problem with our reservation. He offered us a sherry and asked us to wait. Bach's baroque music drifted from hidden loudspeakers. We strolled around the living room: a grand piano; a long white lamé nightdress from the fifties, hanging from a perch; a bird cage with *guacamayas* from Chiapas; chairs upholstered in Damascus silks; a Bufano bronze cast. It was a strange collection of unrelated objects that blended well together.

The desk clerk came up to us. The Gardenia Room was only available for three days. Then, we could pick another room.

"As long as we don't have to change hotels," Genovesa remarked with a smile.

The room was of perfect beauty. We tossed ourselves on the patchwork eiderdown and kissed away the trip's tension. We made love, moaned with delight, laughed and started all over again.

"Ah, but first let me order a bottle of red wine." When our glasses were full we toasted to our freedom. Freedom—the word came with a nervous surge, flump!

The room looked out on the beautiful garden; the scent of flowers filled the air. Nimble clouds were drifting softly across the blue sky. Genovesa suggested we take a long bath. An antique bathtub of gleaming white porcelain stood delicately on its bronze feet. "It's an Empress Josephine tub!" she exclaimed. "How can we miss this!" And with that she undressed, fixed a bath cap on her head and slipped her feet into the water to test if the temperature was right.

"Uy, it's delicious, come on in!" she yelled. "I'm sure I look just like my great-grandmother lying here with this cap on," she said as I walked into the bathroom.

"What a sexy granny she must have been," I joked, sliding down at her side.

Our nervous systems slowed down until they reached their perfect state. Genovesa took off her cap, submerged her head in water and came out smiling like a wet fish.

After three flawless days and nights, the world outside seemed unreal. We half-remembered San Francisco existed: the windy marina, women rolling down soft hills woven in an embrace, the song of wild sea birds.

Only the sea or paintings on the walls of a museum could summon us out of the room. We decided to go to a Motherwell exhibit. My perception had sharpened after these three days. I observed in utter wonder the strength and harmony in the compositions of this contemporary American who had obviously been touched by Latin spirits.

"But you said you didn't like him before we came in," Genovesa recalled.

"I have totally changed my opinion now. What's more, I'm captivated by his way of conveying a sense of infinity."

Genovesa, skeptical at first, as she always was with abstract art, let herself be carried away by my enthusiasm. We came out, exhilarated as if we had just made love. "If Motherwell only knew," I whispered and we laughed joyfully.

As we were walking down the street, I happened to catch sight of a glass box that held free real estate magazines. I stopped and picked one up. The next morning I called several agencies and made appointments for the days that followed.

"It must have a view," I repeated each time as my only imperative.

"And a red brick patio with geraniums, oleander and lady's-slippers...." Genovesa joked sitting next to me on the bed.

Five intense journeys through San Francisco gave us a splendid introduction. We got to know the different barrios, its ethnic groups, the diversity of the people who occupied the hills and the distinct geography of this magical place. We loved the city.

THE HOUSE BY THE SEA

Carol Oriani was standing in the lobby on her strapless spiked heels. The real estate agency had sent its star sales lady to pick us up at the hotel. She had never been to The Mansion before and it seemed to her a place of wonder. Carola was the real name of this big blonde Sicilian, who turned out to be one tenacious Italian woman. After she had taken us to see every place on her list, and expanded our knowledge of the city in more ways than we could thank her, we ended up with the feeling that our case was lost. Then, all of a sudden, she remembered a marvelous place in Sausalito by the ocean and said she would take us there right away.

The flat was built over wooden pillars; there was an ocean view from every room and far in the distance, you could see the hills of San Francisco. If one walked out on the terrace the water was there, at arm's reach.

Genovesa and I embraced each other in bliss. Mrs. Oriani just looked away discreetly. I asked her to please wait outside while we discussed the plans for our future house.

"The sea has to be the axis, don't you think?" I asked, filled with excitement. "The big room will be our bedroom and you can use it as your studio also. For me, we'll fix the small room to work in."

We were delighted. We lay on the rug of the empty apartment and began scheming endlessly.

"Forget it," Genovesa said abruptly, getting on her feet. "This is just a dream, you know that. Your father won't buy you anything until you leave me."

Mrs. Oriani was still waiting outside. A dense fog had descended over the lights on the bay. As we walked out, I was clearly aware that the world was spinning round. I knew that all things would change before the night was over.

I confirmed it when I called my father on the phone that evening. I said I had found the house. His only answer was that I should come back to México immediately. "We can't talk if you're not here," he said.

The following morning, we decided we needed a day off to rest and to think things over. No more touring and no more Carola. Instead, we would take the express bus to Sausalito.

It was very cold and, as the bus pulled in, we had the sudden longing to be in Puerto Escondido. "Such is the paradox of life, my dear," I remarked, smiling. We stepped out onto Bridgeway and walked towards the docks. Handsome yachts swayed in the strong waves. We sat on a wooden raft from which we could glimpse the entire horizon. Genovesa hugged me, whispering in my ear that she wanted a little red wine to warm up. We went to a small shop across the street from the piers. The owners were in the back of the store, so we left on tiptoe with a *Margot Laffitte* 1982 under my coat.

After we drank the first sips I slipped my hand inside Genovesa's green sweater; her skin was warm. She asked me to keep it there, but it was the troublesome hand that caressed without restraint.

The rocking motion made me dizzy. I felt a grip of pain in the pit of my stomach. Sea gulls, with white and gray plumage, drifted in and crowded the docks. Genovesa gave me a sweet kiss on the tip of my nose and ended on my lips. "Mmmm," I mumbled, "but I think we better go. I'm not feeling too well. Let's toast with the remains of our free sample—for strength."

Back in the hotel, I collapsed on the bed. When the pain subsided, Genovesa insisted that she had had enough of Bach's music, Bufanos, and especially of fake American luxuries, and that we should go somewhere else. This time I agreed.

For a change in atmosphere, she chose a hotel in Japantown and we decided to leave right away. We went down to ask for our bill, and while they did the accounting we strolled around Lafayette Park one last time. Back at the cashier's desk, I was startled to see we had spent a small fortune.

"Your American Express has been canceled," said the one with the coif.

"There must be a mistake," I said, slamming the table. They called New York again.

"Your card is *not* accepted," said the up-till-now kind employee. Her tone had changed.

"Ya me chingaron." I put one and one together. "They've just taken my inheritance away."

I imagined myself and Genovesa thrown in jail. My role as martyr rekindled: both of us locked away in an American prison. Genovesa was yellow.

"And what are we going to do now?" she asked with a dry mouth. The way she looked made me giggle. "What are you laughing at? You think this funny?" she asked furiously.

For a few hours we just sat there in the gloomy lobby. No one offered us a sherry. Genovesa finally came up with the idea of calling her Uncle David, who lived in Los Angeles, and borrowing the money.

"David? Wasn't he Ana's great love?" I asked.

"That's him," she nodded.

The next morning we received the check and our skins were saved.

LOST IDENTITY

We arrived in México well after the break of dawn. Genovesa had an early appointment with her dealer so we hardly had any sleep. As she was getting out of bed, I spanked her lightly on her naked bottom and decided I was coming with her. "You go warm up the car while I finish getting dressed," I said.

As I walked into my dressing room I noticed a drawer of the vanity was slightly open. I kept my private journals there and it was always locked, especially when I was away. My heart leapt.

The transgressors had put a ladder up to the second story. They had nonchalantly broken in, gone over my papers and left, without bothering to cover up the traces of their offense. I questioned the cook. She told me that my sons had done it. The act meant a declaration of war.

Luckily, a few days before leaving for San Francisco I had had a couple of dreams. In one of them, my mother was taking away my green Olivetti. "Please," I begged, "I need it to work with." She wouldn't listen to my arguments; she wasn't interested. She left my house, typewriter in hand. In a second dream, my mother ripped away part of a journal. It described in full detail an erotic scene between Genovesa and me. After these two warnings, I had packed a suitcase with the novel and my diaries and taken it to Genovesa's house.

While I was considering the consequences of this ignoble act, Genovesa came running upstairs. She was disheveled. "I started the engine and, all of a sudden, there was a blast."

I had heard enough. I dashed downstairs. A cloud of smoke was rising from the engine. I got out the car Agustín used to drive and took Genovesa to her appointment. I couldn't smile; I had the feeling it would be hard to do so from now on.

191

After she was through, I asked Genovesa to come along with me to the bank. I was trying to convince myself that nothing was as bad as it seemed. But when I got there I found out that my checking account had been reduced to zeros. My father, a former bank owner, had friends there who had illegally taken out all my money. I had to talk to him immediately. I turned to look for a pay phone. When I got through to his secretary she told me he wasn't in.

For hours I tried to get in touch with him, but at dusk I finally realized that he was not going to call me back.

We didn't know what to do, but we decided that Genovesa shouldn't come home with me. It could be dangerous. "Tomorrow, with the light of day, everything will look different," she comforted me. I slept in her studio, and for the first time, didn't rush back to my house at dawn.

The next day, my father still wouldn't return my phone call. I didn't feel like going back to my house alone, so I continued to stay at Genovesa's. I couldn't sleep a wink at night. I started taking sleeping pills and then pills to stay awake. I expected everything to turn out to be a lie. After all, how was it possible that my dearest father could take such terrible measures against me?

Genovesa's apartment became the symbol of the break with my family.

I used to go out walking around the streets of her neighborhood. Everything was so unfamiliar; none of the coordinates in my memory helped me to locate myself. I felt as if I were living in exile. I kept asking myself if this was the freedom I so longed for. And I began to hate it. Humanity seemed terrible.

Genovesa, seeing how bitter and sick I was, suggested I go back home and try to resolve my family affairs from within. "That is precisely what they're expecting me to do," I said. "That I go back, ashamed and humbled, so they can magnanimously restore what they've taken away from me." A sense of dignity rose inside me, the kind known only by those who have been deeply humiliated.

Genovesa quickly set up her apartment. Those empty spaces that had been so meaningful began to crowd with my excesses.

When my children were out at work I went over to my house and, like a thief, took clothes, records, books. Genovesa began to impose a series of restrictions in her house, claiming she needed order to be able to paint. I started to sense I was unwanted. The situation with my family settled into an overwhelming immobility. I felt lost.

One morning, a few weeks later, I was on the brink of despair and decided to call my mother. I wanted her to arrange a meeting with my father. I needed to give myself one last chance to find out what was really going on.

"You have to come see me first and we'll talk," she said. "On that condition only...."

I was afraid of her usual tricks, but I could see no alternative. I accepted.

On my way there, I kept telling myself I had to be cautious, I had to keep my balance. Genovesa had counseled me not to lose my temper.

When I arrived at their house, I found my mother with rollers in her hair and the remains of a papaya beauty treatment still on her face. Not even in the worst of circumstances did she stop worrying about her beauty.

She let me speak without interrupting me. Nothing seemed to surprise her. That my children had infringed on my privacy seemed logical to her; that my father had taken away my money from the bank, logical too. I just had to wait and see how much more he could take away from me.

I pictured myself without a penny from one day to the next and unable to go back to my house. I felt too old and inexperienced to get a decent job. In no time I would be begging for money on a street corner, I thought. Tears sprang to my eyes. When my mother noticed my weakness, she said that some families hired private detectives to find out what dumps their children were living in.

As I listened to the way she spoke, I was certain she had been the one to prompt my sons to break into my private rooms. The fact that I was writing a novel scared her. Above anything else, she feared there would be talk of the family. She always said that to speak against the family was like spitting into one's own eye.

With great effort I managed to keep quiet, but my silence got on her nerves.

"I want to tell you that we know everything," she burst out, holding her head between her hands. I felt the blood drain out of my face.

193

"What is it that you know?" I asked, trying not to show the terror I was feeling.

"That you have sexual intercourse with Genovesa."

The way she said it made it seem so foul. Aj! how could she turn beauty into slime! Now there was no stopping her. She said that I had driven a knife into their flesh.

"And what do you say about your sons? What you did, not even an animal would do!" she cried. "Ay, with all that we gave you!"

I realized I had to leave immediately. Just as I was closing her bedroom door, I heard, "Oh, look at that little girl of mine, what has become of her now?"

I drove back to Genovesa's with tears streaming down my cheeks. A few blocks from her house I ran a red light and a car, racing at full speed, barely missed me. Shaking, I curbed the car into the sidewalk and screamed at the top of my lungs, "Masks off!" I sobbed, feeling that my insides were breaking apart.

THE JEWELS

Months went by and I began to have doubts about my mental health. I was still unable to sleep and tranquilizers didn't help much anymore.

There was an empty lot in front of the studio where homeless men came to sleep at night. One evening, standing by the window, I watched them get into a fight. I saw how one man was bearing all the blows and was being constantly shoved to the ground. He kept trying to defend himself without success.

Genovesa, who I thought was sound asleep, came to stand by my side. "They're drunk," she said and we watched them fight for a long time. In the end, the stronger killed the weaker.

We didn't say a word, just went to bed.

That night, for the first time in months, I slept soundly. When I woke up the next morning, I decided to inspect the scene of the crime. It had all vanished: the discarded chairs and mattresses, the blankets and the dirty pots, even the men were gone. I had the sudden feeling that it had all been a bad dream, and due to a strange association of ideas, the macabre event made me finally accept that I was no longer rich.

"I have no alternative," I told Genovesa, "I must sell my jewels." She tried to comfort me, but in talking we realized that people who own jewels never sell them unless they're in need. "Rich people are never parted from their diamonds. So even if I pretend I'm not, I am poor."

I smeared my face with beauty masks: honey and yogurt first and egg yolk after that. I took a long shower and dried my abundant hair, but much as I tried, I couldn't get myself to look as I used to. "It's too bad," I complained. Genovesa kissed me, claiming I looked beautiful and offered to be my chauffeur. I was grateful, knowing her company made my task easier.

On the way downtown, I tried to convince myself that with the father I had, nobody would question my intentions; not even if they knew I was selling my jewels.

We left the car in the parking lot on López Street, next to all the jewelry stores in the neighborhood. It was infernally hot and Genovesa kept fixing my melting makeup, wiping the black liner from under my eyes.

She was going to wait for me at the bar in the Hotel Ritz, so we ordered *tequilas dobles* to wish me luck. Genovesa tried to appear calm, but I knew better. I was still uncertain as to whom I should visit; my ex-husband, a jeweler, was of course dismissed. After the second drink I decided for the Pretzels, his competitors.

"Is that their real name?" Genovesa asked, surprised.

"No, it's just a nickname. But it suits them well."

I fixed the pleats on my dress and slipped a cinnamon gumdrop in my mouth.

"Now's the time to show them what I've learned in my acting classes!"

"Good luck, love, I'll be waiting for you," she said, raising her glass.

Buby, as his friends called him, came to the door to greet me. It was the first time I had set foot in his establishment and he was pleasantly surprised.

"What good news brings you here?" he asked.

"I want to sell my trinkets," I said with a dismissing gesture of my hand, making them seem worthless. "I'm leaving for Paris and I plan to buy a good piece instead of these *shmattes*."

He seized the opportunity to show me his collection of Bulgari, the Italian jewelry designer. "In case you'd like to have one," he added. One? I'd like to have them all, I thought. When he had gone through the whole series, I told him I was in a hurry and started taking out jewels from the pockets of my jumper. Just then Pretzel, the brother who was four feet tall, came in, looking radiant.

"Have you heard the news?" he asked me.

"No, I haven't," I said.

"I just got a divorce."

"And who did you divorce?"

"What do you mean who? Berta, who else?"

"About time," I said. "Thirty years after, that's news!"

"Now I'll be able to do as I please."

He told me about his apartment in Paris in the XVI Arrondisement.

"Naturally, where else? Perhaps we'll even be neighbors."

"Now all I need is someone young and full of life, ha ha ha..."

This asshole has a lot of opportunities just because he's male, I thought and I hated him. Buby introduced me to the woman who did their appraisals; I tried to catch her eye but she wouldn't look up. I asked her what time the appraisal would be ready. "After lunch," she said and walked away.

Pretzel, the new divorcé, seized the chance to ask me out for lunch. I told him a friend was waiting for me. "It's a pity," he said, disenchanted.

I invited Genovesa to the Prendes, the elegant Spanish restaurant where we always used to go.

"But how will we pay?" she asked. "I don't think we can afford it anymore."

"Don't you worry about anything, okay?"

I was ordering chicken liver sauté, which was the cheapest item on the menu, when the Pretzel brothers came in. I told Genovesa to turn around discreetly.

"Ah, so that's why you wanted to have lunch here, so the jewelers could see you, right?"

"Yes," I nodded.

We were so tense we couldn't talk. When I went back to Pretzel's office, the woman came out of the adjoining room, fanning herself with a little note. She deposited it in front of Buby and he handed it to me without even looking at it. I nearly fainted; the price they wanted to pay was absurd, a total rip-off.

Smiling, Buby said they never bought jewels at retail. I accepted the offer. He paid in dollars *contantes y sonantes*.

I went back to the Ritz carrying myself with a millionaire's air. Genovesa came running to ask me how much they had given me.

"And how do you know they bought them?"

"Because I know you. Where did you put the money?"

"In my back pocket."

"Did they pay you well?"

"So-so."

When I told her the price, she couldn't understand why I was happy.

"Because I'm inviting you out to dance."

"To dance? Where? But we have to take the money home first."

"I invite and you accept...or don't you?"

"And where are you taking me?"

"To the Cueva de La Tigresa."

"What's that?"

"The 'in' place."

She thought the place was a third-class joint and was afraid to walk in. The cabaret was packed with downtown women. Our looks made them curious. A tough lady came over to ask if we were a couple.

"Yes," I said emphatically.

"Well, you're pretty, both of you," she said, and went back to sit with her friends. We sent them a round of tequilas to toast our health. Just then they started playing the song "Oye Salome." Genovesa and I moved to the dance floor. *Oye Salomé, perdónala*....Genovesa put her hand on my butt and asked if I wanted her to take care of it.

"The ass or the money?"

"Both." She hugged me close and we danced until they shut the Cave.

When we got back home I dumped myself on the bed and asked her to take my boots off.

"This is a memorable night," she said, throwing herself over me. I let her make love to me as if I were a white water lily. I didn't notice when I fell asleep.

When I woke up Genovesa was writing in her notebook. She asked if I wanted to hear what she had just written. "This is what I've always wanted: to wake up with someone I love."

DEAR FAFÁ

For two long years I didn't hear from my family. Then one day my father sent an emissary—his half brother, my uncle, an employee in one of his businesses. He wanted to talk to me. My cherished father was bending, he was finally accepting a dialogue. I agreed to meet him at his car agency in the Tlalpan district the following Sunday.

My heart sank to my stomach when I arrived. The music of a lively two-step pounded over the speakers throughout the building. I thought of bullfighters when they are about to step into the arena.

The security guard told me my father was waiting. I saw my reflection in the glass-paneled door and tried to imagine how he would see me. I had changed so much in the past two years.

I sat facing my father across his elegant ebony desk. The first thing I noticed was that he looked old.

Hanging from the wall was a huge photograph of him shaking hands with *el presidente de la República*.

We said hello and I mumbled that I needed to go to the bathroom, urgently. The bathrooms were not open on Sundays and it took him a while to find the right keys.

I was terrified. What was he going to ask me? What was I going to answer? I tried to calm down but my hands were shaking and I had the feeling my blood wasn't flowing properly through my body.

My father, as I expected, came straight to the point. "Your children need you," he said. "Alberto is going to get married soon. How's he going to have the wedding without you? You're not dead."

My father didn't resemble the wrathful man I had known all my life. "You must go back to your duties," he added. "Otherwise you'll regret it."

I didn't know what to say so I kept quiet. Fearing my answers wouldn't be what he expected, he proposed that we take a trip together so we'd have plenty of time to discuss matters.

I accepted without a second thought. I had always loved my father dearly and this could be the opportunity to explain that I had never meant to hurt him; I had never intended to see him or any of the others suffer.

We said goodbye and I left filled with new hopes. Genovesa was waiting for me expectantly. Once I was finished with my chronicle, she asked me not to harbor any illusions until I had listened to what they wanted from me. "You can't just forget the facts—your bank account, the invasion of your privacy, your mother's remarks."

"I can, my memory refuses to remember," I told her. "I'm going on this trip like a child, an unhurt child."

The next day my father called to ask if I had decided where to go yet. I suggested we spend a couple of days at Las Mañanitas in Cuernavaca.

"It's very peaceful there," I said, "and we'll be able to talk."

"No," he said promptly. "I was thinking of going to New York. Two weeks."

Uf! it seemed too far and too long. "All right," I replied.

I had never traveled alone with my father and he had never traveled without my mother. Obviously, the trip would be an event for both of us.

We stayed at the Helmsley Palace. He booked two suites, one for each of us. It had been a while since I had stayed at a five-star hotel and everything appeared superfluous and terribly ostentatious. At bedtime my king-size felt far too wide, and I began to miss Genovesa madly.

The following morning, my father—who was not the kind to waste his time—took me to see the apartment he planned to buy me. It was extraordinary, even more beautiful than I had imagined. But the idea of living there alone filled me with grief. I made no comments.

When he noticed there was no reaction on my part he became impatient. He told the real estate agent—a lady of astonishing beauty—that she would hear from us soon, and we left.

We walked around the streets near the hotel. My father stopped at every store window to look at the elegantly displayed merchandise. We had nothing to say to each other.

When I went to bed in the evening, an alarm system tripped somewhere near the hotel. It rang for hours without end and no one disconnected it. I was desperate. I locked myself in the bathroom, hoping this would shut out the unbearable noise. But it didn't, so I went back to bed.

I had based so many hopes on this trip.

At dawn—with the alarm still ringing—I finally went to sleep.

I dreamt that fluorescent plastic men came flying out of the windows. The narrow streets of Manhattan were filled with these colorful flyers. Dazzled New York residents watched the show from their offices and apartments. When I woke up, the noise was still booming.

After breakfast, I took the bus to Madison Avenue and Eighty-First Street. I strolled around the streets that were familiar. This was a New York that belonged to Genovesa and me.

I hadn't brought my camera on the trip, and now, for the first time, I regretted it. My camera had always been my third eye. It was something that bound Genovesa and me together and kept us aware of the outside world.

Now, without either Genovesa or the camera, I was bored; my eyes did not capture the meaningful things.

I went back to the hotel to meet my father. I knew he didn't like to go out without me and he didn't enjoy my company either. I felt so desolate, my eyes kept filling with tears.

Eight days drifted by in these tedious comings and goings. On Sunday, he suggested we have breakfast in the hotel's wonderful restaurant. Sipping his champagne, he regretted that my mother was alone in México. We both knew how afraid she was of being alone. I suggested he invite her to join us. Later that evening, he announced she would arrive the following day, but first he wanted to talk to me.

We sat in the living room of my suite. He said my mother and he were both old and they would die soon. "We're not important anymore; but Alberto and Ricardo need you…" his voice trailed off.

Throughout his life, this man had felt invincible, and now he was small and trembling. "How could you leave the life you were leading?" he asked. "It's time you go back to what is yours."

I felt deep pity towards my father. I tried to explain that my sons were not children anymore, they were twenty-two and twenty-three. I longed to live *my* life now; it was my turn, it was fair. I wanted to become a writer. I had wished for it all my life.

My father looked out the window. "What kind of strength is this you've acquired with Genovesa?" he asked. "I don't understand." And he walked out of the room. I cried, broken-hearted.

The next day, my mother arrived. We had adjacent suites and I overheard her telling my father that he had a soft head. "If I were you, I would call the police and tell them not to let her out of the States," she said. My father—who was undoubtedly lying on his bed—said nothing.

I wrote a thank-you note, slipped it under their door, and left for the airport to take the first plane back to México.

THE CRANE SINGS

The crane's sad, deliberate step approached. The sound of the wind became more distinct. The crane, maddened by her own craw, gyrated on one leg. She had a fixed eye, a white crest and black body. Her face reminded me of my dead grandmother's—her stiff body lying over the cold stone, her nostrils stuffed with purple cotton. I cried for her death and, to cleanse my feelings of guilt, I slipped into the swimming pool.

Genovesa and I were sunbathing in the exquisite garden of Las Mañanitas. We had taken the weekend off because we both felt we hadn't had time together since I had come back from my trip.

I felt a grimace forming at the sides of my mouth. The crane turned somber. Genovesa, who knew what happened to me at the sight of those birds, implored me not to linger over sad memories. "Come over here, let's swim towards the waterfall," she said, walking towards me. "Don't grieve, that's life, you know?" she added softly.

There was a big commotion among the birds. I had a presentiment that something was about to happen but I tried to calm down. I had to exorcise the images that were haunting me. It was the first anniversary of my grandmother's death.

I stepped out of the pool and sat down to write in my diary. "Shall I get you a sangría?" Genovesa asked loudly from the other side of the pool. "I'd rather have a bull," I said.

It was she who had taught me how to caress my grandmother. Sitting under the shade, I clearly remembered the morning Genovesa came with me to visit her at the nursing home. She had told me, "Don't feel repelled. Take her hand and stroke her hair." My poor grandmother had painfully lifted her head. I was crying. I was suddenly shattered by the realization that my family had forsaken me as I had forsaken her. I asked Bubbe to pray for me, to pray to her God. It was said that she hadn't recognized anyone for years. But she stroked my face. I told her she shouldn't be afraid; she would soon join her mother again. As soon as I said it, I remembered she had never loved her mother. She used to say that her father was a good Jew, with no character, but her mother was a bad person. I told her that her father was waiting for her, and her sisters too. She would not be alone. I doubted whether she understood what I was saying, and I had a sudden feeling that I might be frightening her instead of soothing her. Old age is a curse, I thought.

Now, as the majestic laurel tree swayed its branches above my head, I had the vivid memory of my grandmother just a few months after that visit with Genovesa.

I had found her lounging in her wheelchair, facing the window, her legs covered with a checkered quilt. She was not aware of the forest of ash trees and eucalyptus that moved softly in front of her. She wasn't able to keep her head upright anymore, and soon she wouldn't be able to get out of bed. When she reached this stage, she lay flat in bed, always in the same position, unable to move at all. She moaned softly all the time. I was certain her bones and muscles gave her horrible pain.

She lived like this for a few more years, abandoned in a luxurious hospital without a hint of the world outside. And paradoxically, she, who had never trusted anyone, not even her own blood kin, died in the arms of her faithful nurse. "Be calm, my little girl," the old woman used to say, "I am here to take good care of you."

Genovesa came over with the tall glass in her hand. She placed it on the table. "Cheers, love, stop thinking about death so much and let's go inside. It's getting chilly."

She led me back to our room and invited me into the shower with her. Through her expert amatory arts, she made me forget woes and losses. My family had forsaken me but I was not dead.

AUTUMN ONCE MORE

I had to make a long trip—south, north; north, south—a course along the labyrinths of my mind.

Aunt Natasha had called me in the morning. "Did you know your father is in the hospital with a stroke?"

"It can't be," I said, quivering. The sudden realization of my father's possible death dawned painfully on me. "Nobody called me," I said. I thanked her and hung up with a bad premonition.

Genovesa came into the room but hesitated to ask if there was anything wrong. Tears had sprung to my eyes. Right away she guessed something was the matter with my father.

I dressed in less than ten minutes and left the house in a hurry with Genovesa's "Drive carefully, love" echoing in my ears.

I needed to shut out a few hundred decibels from the outside world. I rolled the window up and covered my neck and ears with the collar of my coat.

I visualized my father's heart in a washbowl, puffing in and out like a soccer ball. He was lying unconscious on an operating table connected to a thousand colored tubes.

I was shocked by the mental picture and switched lanes abruptly. There was a shrieking noise of wheels. Massive crash? no, luckily not...just a loud *"vieja pendeja!"* He was in the right so I apologized.

I looked for a eucalyptus lozenge in the little box which I always carried. I had the strange feeling that time was suspended.

As I was driving past Canal Trece—a local TV station—a sudden downpour began, completely unexpected at this time of year.

At the crossroads of Altavista and Periférico the sewers had turned into rising fountains. Traffic slowed to a turtle's pace. A harsh silence descended on my spirit.

I remembered my father and his friend Paul in Paris. They had been dancing *cassacas*, cossack-style, in a Russian *boite*, holding the tips of white handkerchieves. It hadn't been so long ago....I started to cry.

In front of Gigante, the supermarket in San Antonio Abad, the lime pit sent its fetid vapors up into the air. I looked at myself in the rain-spattered mirror. I've changed a lot over the last few years, I thought. I look like a mature woman now.

I came around the Alencastre circuit until I faced the roller coaster's thousand tiny colored lights. Since my grandmother's death I hadn't seen anybody in the family. I was afraid to meet them again.

I was told at the information desk that my father was in Intensive Care. I stepped into the elevator feeling like I couldn't breathe. None of the family members were in the corridor; it was an incredible opportunity. I opened the door to my father's room; there he was, lying next to a shiny monitor that registered the weak and irregular beat of his heart.

I could hear the cheerful voices of a nurse and doctor in the adjoining room. I was afraid they would walk in any minute and throw me out. I went towards him, shaking. Was he unconscious, or perhaps under the effect of some strong sedative? I couldn't detect what it was; he didn't react to any outward stimuli.

My father looked so weak and old. I realized that just like me, he had been under the illusion that he was immortal.

I wanted to hold his hand but I didn't dare. I walked sadly out of the room and went down to the basement to find my mother. Why hadn't she called me?

She was sitting in the coffee shop surrounded by people who had been informed of my father's condition. She was talking in a high-pitched voice that concealed how vulnerable she felt. I remembered she used to say what a wonderful actress she could be; she could disguise reality so that strangers wouldn't notice her pain, misery or envy.

She gazed at me out of the corner of her eye without showing a sign of surprise. I went over and asked how my father was. Instead of answering she started telling everybody how she had suffered when my father began to feel sick, and still worse, after Brussy had told her he had to be taken to the emergency ward at the hospital. She touched her forehead shaking her head.

"Oh God, please scare us but don't punish us," she said, turning to look at me. "Hearts can't take too much pain," she added, in a mumble.

Naturally this last remark was meant for me, the black sheep. I asked quietly why she hadn't called me.

"Because your father didn't want me to."

"My father didn't want you to?" I didn't believe it.

My sons arrived later from work. They scrutinized me from head to toe and gave me a kiss just to keep face.

Hours went by without anyone coming near me. I felt like one of those poor relatives who everyone tries to avoid. I went into the bathroom and cried for a while. I made up my mind to stay until I found out what my father's condition really was.

My brother and sons were constantly going in and out of his room while I stood alone in the hall. I wanted to see him before leaving but my mother said my presence might disturb him. When I said goodbye at midnight my brother stood in the threshold with his arms akimbo and threatened me. "Don't you dare go in or I'll kill you!" he yelled.

I left the hospital with a painful realization. I had taught my sons to adore and respect my father as if he was their own and now they acted like merciless judges—just like him.

I sped through the empty city streets. When I got home Genovesa was still up, waiting.

"I was so worried...how is he? I'm glad you're back."

GRAND FINALE

Genovesa and I went to live in Paris. This had been the dream of every artist from my generation and from hers too. But things didn't turn out as they do in dreams.

Genovesa met a man who fell in love with her. Months later he proposed and she decided to marry. She wanted to have children, a home; a normal life. She left for the United States to live in a small town in Colorado. I stayed behind, broken. Loneliness devoured me mornings, evenings and nights.

Little by little, I managed to write again and the novel of our love kept growing.

A few years later, Genovesa wrote me a letter saying she wanted to visit me.

On the morning of her arrival I went out to buy red roses, her favorite flowers. The florist whom I hadn't visited in years was astounded; she thought I had gone back to my native country. At home, I set the flowers in the entrance hall, in a vase under a halo of artificial light.

Due to one of those twists of fate, I was writing the last chapter of the love story we had lived together. Clarity flowed unrestrained as I sat in front of the computer, so I decided not to pick her up at the airport; I'd surprise her with the finished manuscript instead. After all, this book had been a dream we shared.

Genovesa arrived and rang the doorbell. When no one came to answer, she took out the old set of keys she had kept and opened the entrance door to the building. The taxi driver helped her with the suitcases.

As she came into the hall she noticed the flowers and found the card I had written. 'I love you,' it said.

She thought it was strange that I didn't come out to welcome her, but knowing me as she did, she figured it was one of my jokes.

*She entered the living room. Nothing had really changed. Her
paintings still hung on the wall; there were the photographs, the
Venetian windows she adored. It had been our home for years; now
it was only mine.*

*She stood by the window and watched the street. Everything
looked so familiar. It was winter but there were leaves on the maple
tree. Strange music was streaming from my studio. She knocked on
the door but there was no answer. She opened it quietly and saw
me slumped over my desk. She approached without making a noise.
On the page she read...*

*'Valeria was dead. Her mother's curse had been fulfilled. She
died alone and deserted by all.'*

The End

The ending of the novel was dramatic but it seemed nothing
compared to the one my family was planning for me.

My mother, brother and children had openly accused me of
being the cause of my father's health condition. The doctors had
diagnosed the stroke as a result of his sedentary life and the
sybaritic abuses of the old man. But to them that had no importance. I had to endure the worst insults, furious hatred, even
threats to my life. Grief-stricken, I watched the beastly demonstra-
tions of their power. The process was so painful that by the time
I realized everything was over between us, I felt relieved.

I ripped up the last pages I had written about my own death
and took a deep breath. I was conscious that the ending of the
novel and reality had come close together. I decided the best
thing to do was to leave the country. My life with Genovesa could
not flourish, my writing would be stifled. I remembered Morena's
words when I first met her, "a Mexican in exile." That's what I was
about to become.

A BLUE SEA
OF NOSTALGIA

This is the spoken picture of a white room. Intricate blues and greens under an intense sky. Genovesa is standing by the window looking at the Aegean Sea. She calls me to her side, she wants to talk about the light. "When I paint, light is most important to me," she says.

"I know what you mean."

We turn to the mirror on the wall. It reflects our images: two naked bodies. She is darker than I am, more Semitic. Our differences in age are obvious. She embraces me, saying that this had been her dream. She had to live it through to know what it was like.

I photograph the window through the mirror: the two of us kneeling before one another, kissing. Two mouths touching, click. We catch the ocean's shimmer in reflection. The light of a sinking sun fills the room; trapezoids and golden circles appear. Our shadows split into fragments on the white wall.

She pours wine for me from the untamed regions of Greece. Far in the distance a steamer leaves port. We listen to the mysterious song of its pipes; I imagine vignettes of smoke blowing from its chimneys. We kiss. "I love you," I say.

"I love you too."

Three sea birds fly across the window. We make love listening to the waves breaking against the cliff where the house is anchored.

When night falls she wants to go out into the open.

"No more walls around us, I want an open view of the Aegean," she exclaims.

We put on the clothes that lie scattered around the bed and go out onto the esplanade.

"Siete, aldaba, pez," I yell. "Seven, latch, fish."

"You and me, seven years together," she says.

We sit on the benches outside the wine shop under the naked sky. The notes of a guitar fade in the wind. A few men dressed in white are singing traditional melodies. Women with velvety eyes keep them silent company. We toast to all good loves.

Suddenly we hear a tinkling of broken glass coming downhill. A prehistoric animal appears on the summit. Its tail strikes the burning rocks.

"A propitious sign," I say. Genovesa sets her glass aside.

"You know, I finished reading your novel this morning. I like it. Very much," she says.

I pull a crumpled piece of paper, with a Spanish letterhead, out of my skirt pocket and read out loud, "We're happy to inform you that your book has been accepted for publication...."

"When did you receive that?" she asks, forcing the letter out of my hand.

"This morning," I reply with a guilty smile.

"So that's what you meant—a 'propitious sign', eh? Viva México!...what's the matter love? Suddenly your face is sad."

"México brings back painful memories; you know what a high price I had to pay...and you...."

"Do you regret it?"

"Oh, no...no. Freedom is too precious; I know I couldn't write without it."

"But you still wonder if everything could have been different, right?"

"If I knew then what I know now...but life isn't like that, is it?"

"So then, shall we toast to freedom?" Genovesa picks up her glass again. I raise mine.

"Yes, but better yet, let's toast to the day when all women can love freely." We clink our glasses.

The sounds harmonize, break, fade. The sea, again, comes into focus. The linear turns concentric.

GLOSSARY

Abuela — Grandmother

aj! — ugh!

añil — a particular shade of bright-blue housepaint used in México and in Caribbean countries

Anís del Mono — Spanish anise drink

ata la rata; Maja es Maya — play on sounds in Spanish

Ay! los hombres! — Oh! Men!

La bella — The beauty

boleros — romantic Mexican love songs

cachucha — cap

café con leche — coffee with milk

calvados — an alcoholic drink common in France

cantinas — bars where strictly alcohol is served

carey — tortoise shell

cementera — a cement factory

ché — Argentinian word used to address someone affectionately

chupa — Hebrew; a wedding canopy

churros — long pieces of deep-fried dough dipped in sugar

La colonia — the barrio or district

con lujo de detalle — with every detail

constantes y sonantes — cash

las cosas del corazón — affairs of the heart

de gorrón — to eat or drink at other's expense

deshabillez-vous vite — undress fast

Dia de Muertos — The Day of the Dead

duro y dale — one time after another

ensabanado Fantomas — putting the cape on Fantomas; a playful saying which is a pun on the word *sabanas*, or sheet, used here to refer to rolling papers as well as to the customary cape worn by Fantomas, a Mexican cartoon character from the 1960's much like Superman

extramuros — outside the walls

Frenesi — the name of a song; means 'ravishing passion'

habitues — from French; habitual or customary

huevona, huevonzota, huevoncita — a lazy bum

ipso facto — from Latin; right away, immediately

jacaranda — a crawling-vine flower of very bright colors

joven — a young man

llamaradas — from 'llama'-flame. A deep orange-colored flower

loro — a green parrot

Los muy cabrones — 'the sons-of-bitches'; derogatory usage of '*cabrón*', or he-goat

manita de puerco — to force the hand forwards at the wrist violently

medias de seda — literally 'silk stockings'; a light alcoholic drink popular among teen-age girls

Michoacán — a state in central Mexico, Northwest of Mexico City. Capital: Morelia. Population: 3.5 million

oaxacavidamia — idiomatic expression meaning 'Oh! my God!' (literal translation: 'Oaxaca—my life')

ocote — an especially flammable type of wood used to start fires

oy vey is mir — Yiddish expression for 'woe is me'

palmeras borrachas de sol — words from a popular romantic song meaning 'palm trees drunk with the sun'

peña — a club specializing in Latin-American music

pendeja, pendejo — 'asshole'

percherón — a draft horse

pinguina — penguin

Puente de Muertos — the holiday celebrating the Day of the Dead

putane, ritornate a l'Italia! — Italian; tramps, go home! (back to Italy)

puto — usually means 'fag'; here used to mean 'son-of-a-bitch'

shmatte — from Yiddish: something old, cheap or discarded

sui generis — from Latin: something of its own peculiar kind; in a class of its own

tacón y punta — heel and toe

tan naca — silly

te cebo un matecito — to steep the mate leaves for tea: an expression used only in South America where mate is drunk

Televisa — Mexico's private television network

tortas — Mexican version of a sandwich; always with beans, salsa or chile and made on bolillo, a crusty white roll

un as del volante — an ace driver

un taco de buche y otro de ojo — tacos made from pig's neck and eyes

Valeria querida, Valeria adorada — dear Valeria, adored Valeria

ya me chingaron — they screwed me up

zapatillas de charol — dress shoes made of patent leather

zempasúchiles — orange flowers used for altar and tomb offerings on the Day of the Dead

zócalo — central square

SARA LEVI CALDERÓN was born and raised Jewish in México City. She married, gave birth to two children, got divorced, became a sociologist, and then fell in love and learned the wonders of becoming a lesbian.

After all this, she dared to become a writer.

aunt lute books is a multicultural women's press that has been committed to publishing high quality, culturally diverse literature since 1982. In 1990, the Aunt Lute Foundation was formed as a non-profit corporation to publish and distribute books that reflect the complex truths of women's lives and the possibilities for personal and social change. We seek work that explores the specificities of the very different histories from which we come, and that examines the intersections between the borders we all inhabit.

Please write or phone for a free catalogue of our other books or if you wish to be on our mailing list for future titles. You may buy books directly from us by phoning in a credit card order or mailing a check with the catalogue order form.

Aunt Lute Books
P.O. Box 410687
San Francisco, CA 94141
(415) 558-8116